#7 - nice chapter
p. 51 - nice touch

for Suzi

The Mules that Angels Ride.

Page Edwards, Jr.

A Howard Greenfeld Book

J. Philip O'Hara, Inc.
Chicago

Library of Congress Cataloging in Publication Data

Edwards, Page.
    The mules that angels ride.

    I. Title.
PZ4.E264Mu [PS3555.D95]   813'.5'4   70-188737
ISBN 0-87955-900-4

J. Philip O'Hara, Inc.   20 East Huron, Chicago, 60611.
Published simultaneously in Canada by Van Nostrand Reinhold Ltd.,
Scarborough, Ontario.

First Printing G
"Le Monocle de Mon Oncle," by Wallace Stevens, from COLLECTED
POEMS, by Wallace Stevens. © 1954 by Wallace Stevens. Reprinted
by permission of Alfred A. Knopf, Inc.

The mules that angels ride come slowly down
The blazing passes, from beyond the sun.
Descensions of their tinkling bells arrive.
These muleteers are dainty of their way.
Meantime, centurions guffaw and beat
Their shrilling tankards on the table-boards.
This parable, in sense, amounts to this:
The honey of heaven may or may not come,
But that of earth both comes and goes at once.
Suppose these couriers brought amid their train
A damsel heightened by eternal bloom.

Wallace Stevens,
"Le Monocle de Mon Oncle"

Then the ends of the tent fell outward and down,
and the circus of Doctor Lao was over. And into
the dust and the sunshine the people of Abalone
went homewards or wherever else they were going.

Charles G. Finney,
The Circus of Dr. Lao

I.

Chapter one.

1. Monatti.

A lone man with a scar on his right cheek that cut from his ear to his lip jumped from the back of a pickup truck and walked toward Lupine's Bar and Grill in Rio Barranca. He carried a leather satchel with a flat-bladed spade strapped to its side.

Lupine was sitting at the counter reading the paper, the scar startled her.

"Digger Monatti."

"You dug before, Mr. Monatti?"

"Yes."

"Six feet. You fill them in after the service."

"Yes, Ma'am."

"You make straight edges?"

"Yes, Ma'am," Monatti smiled.

"Well, go talk with Art Blackstone. If it's all right with him, you can consider yourself hired." After the man had gone, she said, "Wheew. He's a mean looking one."

No one considered making arrangements in Albuquerque as they had in the past after Art Blackstone
moved to Rio Barranca. Coroner, undertaker, town
florist, he had closed his home in Salem, Oregon,
and installed his office in the shell of an old house
surrounded by cottonwood trees on Verde street in
Rio Barranca. The front section of the house, which
had been the living room, held the flowers and
chairs for customers. The embalming room had been
the downstairs bedroom and bath. The visiting room
was the old den immediately off the flower room.
Art lived upstairs. He had covered the downstairs
floors with tile and installed drains in the rooms. In
his offices, he could embalm, perform an autopsy,
make-up, encase, dress, and load the deceased. He
also cared for the burial records at the cemetery,
decorated for weddings, and gave the extra flowers
to the church. A soft-spoken, gentle man, the undertaker had infused himself into the community with
care and cunning.

"Have you any experience?" Blackstone asked.
He was working on an old lady.

"I dug in Oakland, Pomona, Long Beach, and
Fort Worth before going to San Francisco."

"We have different ground out here."

"So I noticed."

"It's hard going and there ain't much pay."

"There never is."

"If you run out of things to do, you can always
clip weeds. See that you keep the grounds watered
and the gate locked when you aren't around."

"I didn't hear anything about the pay."

"Your room is free, there is a cottage up at the gate. We pay two dollars an hour for ground work. We pay twenty-five a grave. That means digging and filling both." Blackstone handed him the key. "You will find the cemetery about six blocks north. Say, Monatti, glad you came when you did. Old Mrs. Slate here goes in on Friday morning. I have already staked the hole, thought I might have to go down myself."

Digger took the key. It was a nice morning. Birds, sun, high cumulus clouds. The caretaker's cottage had a three-quarter bed, bath, shower, kitchen. Digger liked showers. The tool shed was attached to the rear. *nice writing. Smooth, easy. A story teller at work.*

edaphic - relating to soil, especially as it affects living organisms

stroboscopic - (strobe) high-intensity short-duration light pulses; makes moving objects appear stationary

2.   The first *edaphic fuse.

At noon in a large Eastern city the light from the sun turned stroboscopic. A large majority of the people were on their lunch hour at that moment and dressed very fine. The*stroboscopic sun made most of them feel as though they had the chance to be on the cover of a long-playing record album. A few people went so far as to croon to the sun while others made long arching leaps off the curbstones or put their heads together to form groups all making sequences of serious or slapstick faces.

A few others were seen stealing into the public library or sitting in the back of underground magazine stands. Robert Quinn deposited a token in the subway entrance at Twenty-third street and Park Avenue south and sat it out on a bench reading from a recently formed ecology newspaper, *Earth*. Aside from the city's daily paper, *Earth* was Quinn's favorite reading material.

12

3. Blow pipe and ⃰cupel.

Pfizer Lawrence bent close over his blowpipe, he
dropped a measure of borax on the heated oxide he
was working with. "Ah, ha." The bead turned blue.
"Cobalt. Twenty-seven. One four nine five degrees
Centigrade," he said.

The laboratory bell sounded.

Chuck Swanson of Swanson's Hardware in Rio
Barranca held a bottle before Pfizer. "Martin wants
another test."

Pfizer's protective glasses made him look like a
bug.

"He is certain it tastes like raw sewage this time."

The shack was hot and smelled like a mixture of
boiling ammonia and sulphuric acid. Pfizer didn't
believe in modern soaps and did his washing under
plain hot water. He worked up a sweat when the
furnace was going, and the smell gave Swanson the
sensation that all the hairs in his nose were being

singed. He found he could breathe most comfortably in short gasps.

"Fifteen a test," said Pfizer. "Martin understand that?"

Swanson nodded, he had removed himself to the far end of the laboratory by the windows.

The chemist shut off the gas and oxygen jets on the blowpipe and prepared for the water test. He replaced his black protective glasses with his usual pair and peered at Swanson over the wire rims. "Do you know what I think?" He spoke in a harsh whisper, "I think Martin Walters is obsessed. He doesn't really care what he drinks as long as he knows what it is.

"Once Lupine fed him a black and white soda with the milk gone bad, and he said, 'What's this?' Lupine tasted it and said, 'A black and white soda but the milk's gone bad.' And, by God, he drank the son of a bitch."

chuckle

The front section of Pfizer's clapboard building was his living quarters. At the rear, his laboratory hung out over the river bank on long cedar supports. A trail passed alongside the building before it began a series of switch-backs down the steep bank to the Barranca river. Pfizer had built the lab with lots of windows. What he couldn't see from his front porch swing he could from his laboratory. Once, sometimes twice, a week he fired up the furnace and filled it with small bone ash cupels. He was sure, fast, and asked no questions. He kept the place just clean enough so not to get the samples mixed.

14

"Say, Chuck. I hear old Bicycle Lena's come down with her delusions again. Old Lena, crazier than a coot."

"I saw her a while ago wheeling a load of groceries over to her place. Looks to me like she's setting up for a long one this time. She had more groceries than I've seen her with in a long time. Couldn't ride. Had to wheel herself home."

"Hell of a waste. She's a mighty pretty lady when she works at it. As good-looking or better than her daughter." Pfizer continued to move about the laboratory. "It's a wonder she can keep that shop of hers going."

"All I know," said Swanson, "is she has got herself an angel in that Swede girl, Ingrid. That girl can run the shop better than Lena herself."

A few of Pfizer's steady customers thought he brought them luck, and they kept coming back to him with rocks. Others thought he might find a trace of gold to spirit a sinking heart, and they, too, kept coming to him with rocks. A man of precision, Pfizer had the knack of uncovering a slight trace of lead or silver or zinc or, most frequently, gold in almost every sample. He told no lies, worked close, and could read a borax bead better than most. In all, it kept the business coming through the door.

"What you working on these days?"

"Business or pleasure?"

"Pleasure."

"Pottery glazes and aphrodisiacs."

Pfizer shoved his glasses back up his nose, they

datura - plant with large trumpet-shaped flowers.

magnified his eyes into huge watery orbs. "Hee. Hee." His was a nervous laugh. "They haven't ever made a real one you know. One that gives her more than an itch." He turned from the counter to face Swanson. "Do you realize even the Indian's *datura* will harm a lady? Hee. Hee."

He had poured some water into a vial and was holding it over a burner. He measured a small quantity in a burette on the lab table. "Did you hear about the man from Dayton. A crazy millionaire, he was developing a permanent aphrodisiac. The ASPCA caught up with him. Hee. Hee. He was trying it out on dogs. They say the noise in his place is what gave him away."

Pfizer had completed the test and was scribbling on a note pad. "The first time Walters had me walking up to the reservoir myself. A bill for fifty changed his tune."

Pfizer handed the results to Swanson. "If he thinks those people are shitting in the town water, why doesn't he drill himself a well. All he needs is a dowser, and there are plenty of them around if you know where to look."

"That so?"

"Sure. Tell Martin I'll do a culture if he wants me to."

burette -
(byoŏ-rĕt')
a uniform-bore glass tube with fine graduations and a stopcock at the bottom, used especially in laboratory procedures for accurate fluid dispensing and measurement.

16

4. Bicycle Lena.

On the first day there was a rain of frogs, serpents,
lizards, scorpions, and many venomous beasts of that
sort. On the second, thunder was heard, and light-
ning and sheets of fire fell upon the earth, mingled
with hail stones of marvellous size; which slew
almost all, from the greatest even to the least. On
the third day there fell from heaven a stinking
smoke, which slew all that were left of men and
beasts, and burned up all the cities and towns in
those parts. (De Smet, 1348)

Wrapped in a dark shawl, she chained her bicycle to
a post outside her apartment house, and carrying
two huge bags of groceries she climbed the stairs. A
thin woman, suspicious and dry, Lena Romero
owned the Road Runner Shop in Rio Barranca and
lived alone with her cat, Dr. Dee. Lena had a
daughter, Purty, who lived in Rio Barranca, but they
did not speak to one another. The day that Lena

17

learned Purty had been sleeping with Lou Willis on the banks of the Barranca river was the day that Lena disowned her. Lena now lamented her daughter out of habit, for the sake of the salvation of Purty's, as well as her own, soul.

Her house was old and was in the old section of Rio Barranca, a few streets from the river. Adobe walls, mud-packed floors sealed with concrete, water and steam pipes traversing the ceiling. Lena lived on the second floor. Indian rug. Low pine table. Chairs covered with red plastic. Tight kitchen. The most elaborate furnishing was the bookcase which had glass doors. An apothecary jar and mortar and pestle rested on the top. The books were old and dark, water-stained, folk medicine books, ragged from use. None of the titles were familiar to the common eye. An extensive selection of roots and herbs were arranged on the bookcase's lower shelves. Among the clutter was a heart-shaped amulet banded with silver on a chain. The bed, a huge four-poster constructed of notched beams and pegs, could be adjusted to almost any height, and a dark canopy could be lowered to seal the occupant within.

Lena poured a cup of tea and sank onto the bed. She felt feverish. Her head ached, her eyes were fiery red, she looked half drunk. Symptoms. Her tongue was swollen. She shivered constantly. The delirious plague visions were beginning to occur. There would be no epidemic in Rio Barranca. Lena, the unfortunate woman, would be the sole victim.

She climbed into bed and pulled the canopy closed, Dr. Dee woke and spoke to her.

Said the cat, "You are sick again, My Lady. I have called two friends to come attend you. You will remember them, for they have been here before. Peck the Beak Doctor and Licket. They will be here soon."

Rats, black rats infested the town. Lena's head began to buzz, for days the rats had been scurrying just beyond her sight behind doorways into cellar windows. She could hear them squeal, she could feel them thick and moving behind the walls.

"I would not go out onto the street, My Lady," said Dr. Dee. "The Beak Doctor will impose a quarantine for you."

She could hear them scramble in the gutters. She could never have walked the streets alone, for lodged firmly in her mind was the sound of the crushing skulls beneath her feet. She could not have moved from the bed were she asked to.

"I will be leaving you now, My Lady. Licket will take my place. When you have recovered, I will return."

Dr. Dee, purring at Lena's last caress, grasped his tail in his mouth and began to walk around the bed to set up his spin. When his turning began to disturb the bed covers, he lifted himself and spun in the air. His disappearance startled Lena momentarily, for Dr. Dee had successfully transformed himself into a bright ring of light and vanished through a tiny hole in the bed's dark canopy.

Shortly afterwards, Licket entered through the same hole in the canopy with a cedar stick in his mouth. He did not disturb Lena when he curled at the foot of the bed to wait.

5. The second edaphic fuse.

Most everyone in the city carried large brightly colored plastic umbrellas. As the crowds grew larger many of the umbrellas were jabbed and crushed to such an extent that they became ineffective. At midday and in the early evening a number of people whose umbrellas had been crushed could be seen trying to grab or at least get under umbrellas not belonging to them. People came to rely on their plastic umbrellas very much. When the manufacturers could not produce them rapidly enough, causing the price to skyrocket, those with no umbrellas began the age-old ruse. A clever person learned quickly to transform himself into a convincing luxuriant brightly colored replica of those same large plastic umbrellas. Those who pulled the ruse carefully and with aplomb did astonishingly well for themselves on an informal rental basis.

Chapter two.

6. Estelle's tattoo and Happy Dan.

Huge billboards which read *Snakes Live!, Rattlers'*
Nest, Cactus Cool Ade, Curios had been set up along
the roads outside of Las Vegas, Dallas, Denver,
Cleveland to attract visitors to Martin Walter's snake
museum in Rio Barranca. A small concrete block
curio shop with a rattlesnake pit on the outskirts of
town, the museum was a tribute to Martin's dead
wife Jenny, who was known professionally as Izella
the Snake Lady. A number of the rattlers that Jenny
had used in her show lived in the pit, they were
Martin's living memorial for dead Jenny, and he saw
they were well cared for. Dan and Estelle Anderson,
the museum's husband and wife management team,
lived in a trailer house close by, and they knew
about snakes. Estelle once had a show of her own,
she had been Jenny's friend as well as her rival.

The museum's curio shop sold most of the same
things Lena Romero did in the Road Runner Shop
in town. Leather moccasins, lap robes, tomahawks,

drums, all direct from the crate at slightly lower prices. In one corner of the building were the mementos. A mongoose that was allegedly killed by a cobra, an impressive collection of stuffed snakes, Jenny's first python, Hydra, a cobra snake, and a few anacondas that she had in her show, as well as a short narrative and appreciation written by Martin himself with accompanying blow-ups of Izella the Snake Lady in her tight costume filled the museum's "Snake Lady Relic Corner." The corner was Martin's idea, he thought Jenny would like to be remembered that way. The Cactus Cool Ade, an exotic vegetable drink served in a replica of a Saguaro cactus, was Estelle's. For the approaching season, Martin had planned a new wrinkle. Hobbled and harnessed to a tractor wheel, a buffalo grazed behind a board fence out back of the building.

Martin spent a fair amount of his time in the museum. He stood over the display cases in the relic corner and consulted with Estelle. He told her about Jenny, and as time passed they had begun to carry on a mild flirtation in the reflection of the glass display cases.

Estelle wore low-cut dresses during their consultations, for she knew Martin liked to catch glimpses of her red and blue rattlesnake tattoo. She would bend over the display case allowing him to see the red tongue flicking from the snake's mouth. Estelle was a natural dancer, and when she wanted to she could move like she was rubbing herself up against something that she definitely approved of, a steel

26

fire pole maybe. And every time Martin saw her moving that way, he thought of the tattoo going along with her on her belly, and it set something off inside him. Even in the early days when Jenny was young Estelle could always light him up inside. She had danced for Martin only once, long ago, but he found himself beginning to hope that she might one day dance for him again.

As for Estelle's husband, Happy Dan Anderson, no one saw much of him. He was sickly and kept to the trailer house caring for his Siamese cats. Sometimes at night, Happy Dan would emerge from the trailer and turn on the floodlights. He would stand in the gravel drive of the snake museum in his white jacket, bush hat, cracking his bull whip at imaginary beings on the drive. He looked, then, like an escaped billboard illustration magnified in the lights, his whip spraying gravel against the board fence.

In Rio Barranca, Dan wouldn't let Estelle run free the way she was used to. He watched her from the trailer, kept her from the car keys, and suspected early on that something was up with Martin Walters. For too many years she had drug him around like a cardboard cutout and propped him next to her at bars all across the country. He had spent half his life cocking his elbow next to her while she, the most attractive woman many small bars had ever seen, pushed up against strangers after her dance number. When they went off the road, Happy Dan went moral. He forbid her to dance. Most people who met Estelle could see she was aching to be set free from howling, half crazy Happy Dan, the most harmless person in Rio Barranca even when he was cracking his bull whip at light spots in the road.

7. The third edaphic fuse.

In the city, those who had no place in the country could be seen at various times rolling in the leaves in the city's many parks. The recreation, sponsored by the Parks Department, was called "Going to the Leaves."

People made inquiries such as: "Have you been to the Leaves?" "Will I see you at the Leaves?" Or statements: "Why, I am certain I saw you at Leaves myself." The city's Promotional Experts made declarations: "Going to the Leaves is better than two things." "Everybody goes to the Leaves."

Though the idea met with certain success, a number of people were repelled by the Leaves. They had too many memories, and they knew the Leaves were manufactured from aluminum and silica. They refused to make contact with unnatural substances.

Robert Quinn begrudgingly went to the Leaves two or three times a week. He, along with a few others,

29

gritted his teeth, buttoned up around the collar, and rolled because he knew it was good for him even though the Leaves didn't even sound like the real item.

One evening after Leaves, Quinn found a small bar that served exotic hamburgers as well as generous drinks. He usually went to a bar after Leaves, and the Masque Bar that evening seemed as good a choice as any. A few leaves would always be left sticking in Quinn's hair, that particular evening was no different except the lights in the bar struck the leaves in such a way to cause small light beads to be reflected onto the ceiling. The light beads danced and twirled to the movements of Quinn's head as he drank his whiskey.

A girl, fascinated by the reflections, opened a conversation by asking him if he had been at the Leaves. She said though she had not been there that particular evening, she was certain she had seen him at Leaves once and, aside from that, did he know he still had leaves in his hair and that they were making the most marvelous patterns on the ceiling.

When Quinn looked up to see, the lights smashed in the girl's eyes, and she pretended to be very dazzled and offered to help remove the leaves from his hair before he blinded someone.

At this point it is important to mention that both Robert Quinn and the girl, Katie, as well as every other patron in the bar, the waiters, bartender, and hat check girl were wearing masks, small masks that covered the nose, cheeks, and a portion of the upper

30

lip. This mask, though it covered only a small fraction of a person's face, could make unhappy eyes, teary eyes, glazed eyes, all look very happy. It was a most remarkable mask, and a most remarkable thing to receive in a bar. It is impossible to describe what that mask could do to a set of happy eyes. When anyone entered the Masque Bar, he was given a mask. The bar had many loyal patrons who declared it the most delightful place in town.

Katie and Quinn moved to a corner and began to converse. They had an exotic hamburger, and after a time agreed they should leave the place together and go out onto the street. After the hamburgers, *nice* both were dazzled and looked happy as pie. Quinn *sentence* paid the bill, and they went for their coats.

The lady at the coat room asked them if they would mind returning their masks to the mask box. In silence, they left the bar and walked the street for what seemed to them like blocks, they did not look into store windows and could hardly bring themselves to lift their faces from the sidewalk to check the street lights. Quinn set a pace much faster than Katie was used to and once she, as they stepped down a curb, tripped and would have fallen before a taxi if Quinn had not caught her. He caught her, and he looked at her face.

She had one very large tear in the corner of her eye, but otherwise her face was radiant. She smiled even wider when she saw Robert's smile. And he smiled wider still. The mask had left its mark, and they walked thirty-seven blocks that night looking at each other and escalating in the happiness behind one another's smile.

nice chapter

8.   Memorial services.

The wind from Rio Barranca whipped like fire over
the top of cemetery hill, bending the dry grass flat
against the slope. With his flat-bladed spade, Digger
Monatti carefully cut the rectangle and rolled the
grass back on a long piece of damp burlap. He
spread a canvas for the dirt and began his descent.
    The anxious moment came and went,
    No wood or bone at four and a half feet.
When the crown of his hat met the grave's edge, he
rested a moment before trimming the hole.
    There are seven ways of getting out of a grave:
1) place your shovel across the width of the grave at
the top and, using it as a chinning bar, in one
smooth motion lift your body onto the shovel's
handle and move from a position over the grave onto
the grass; 2) vault with the shovel out of the grave,
being certain the handle is left tilted against the side
so you can bend down and retrieve it; 3) pull a
short ladder into the grave and climb out, retrieving

it either by hand or with a hook attached to the
end of a rope; 4) rely on spectators or assistants to
lift you out; 5) compose a ladder from the shovel
and retrieve it when you are out; 6) pound stakes
into the grave's walls and climb up, kicking them
out as you make your ascent so the coffin will not
knock against them; 7) dig a series of holes in one
corner up the side for your hands and feet,
remembering before you leave to clean the dirt out
of the bottom of the grave.

Digger leaned his flat-bladed spade against the side
of the hole. He unscrewed a cap in the top of the
handle and extracted four aluminum rods and a
five-foot length of nylon cord. He fixed the rods
into the shovel's handle and attached the cord to his
belt and the handle loop. He then sank the blade
into the grave's bottom and climbed out, pulling his
shovel behind him.

Irma Slate's funeral was scheduled for eleven. The
cemetery's masterplan placed her at the far end of
the long, narrow Slate Plot. Slate money and Slate
tradition declared each couple was to be buried side
by side in a line, heels forward, beginning with the
Old Slates in the front at the west edge of the
cemetery.

The five children were lined up, heels first,
behind according to age. Irma's slot was in the
middle, and hers was the last grave in the Slate
family. The next freshest was her father's up front,
she had cared for him many years after her mother

died. Were the Creator, as Old Slate always dreamed,
to exhume the clan en masse and march them away
to the west, the Old Slates in the lead, Irma would
walk alone with no warm arm to tuck hers under,
with no man's trousers-leg for her skirt to brush
against in the dry wind. Old Slate had been ruthless
in his affection for Irma Slate, and she unremitting
in her loyalty.

Purty Romero had worn a thin frock to the
memorial service. The skirt was nearly short enough
to be bad taste. She knew about the new attendant
and afterwards peeked into the window of the
caretaker's shack. A man with a mustache interrupted by a scar that cut from his ear to his lip
stared out at her. She looked in again wide-eyed. He
was so young. When she saw him the second time,
outside the shack, her belly shook with a spasm. As
he stood there talking with the undertaker, she could
do little more than finger the button on her blouse.

"Good going, Monatti," said Art Blackstone. "We
haven't seen a better hole in years. Myself, I like a
tight fit. That box slipped down there just as nice as
could be. You are a man after my own heart. Good
going, Monatti."

The grave digger's presence assaulted Purty. No
one had robbed her of wit and breath like that since
she had first laid eyes on Lou Willis. Her husband,
dead.

While he talked with Blackstone, Monatti watched
Purty. He let her know that he was thinking. He

could see her flesh, pink and fresh and soft. He
knew all he had to do was wait.

Monatti filled the hole, set the Widow Slate's stone,
tamped the fresh earth, rolled the grass back onto
the mound, and placed some flowers in a couple of
coffee cans. The headstone had come from storage,
only the date had to be cut in. Old Man Slate had
ordered an even dozen stones, the twelfth would not
be needed. The decorations on all the stones were
the same. They all were topped with a life-sized
hand with its index finger pointing straight up.

9. Peck the Beak Doctor.

Men now coolly ventured on what they had formerly done in corners. (Thucydides, 430 B.C.)

No human saw a slender man enter Lena Romero's apartment carrying a large black bag and a thin cane as light as a wand. He had entered the sweet, motionless air of her canopied bed without disturbing it.

"My Lady," said Licket sitting at the edge of the bed. "Peck the Beak Doctor is here to examine you."

His huge elongated nostrils curved inwards from either side as smooth as a mask. His oilcloth cloak was dark. His cap, designed as a mask with mica sheets fit in the eye holes and a long bill, was lined with oils, herbs, and other antidotes. The sight of the doctor cheered Lena.

When she spoke she could not be heard by human ears. Hello Doctor. It is very nice to see you once again. I think I am very ill.

37

bubo – an inflamed swelling of the lymphatic gland, especially in the area of the armpit or groin. (bubonic)

When she told him of her shivering, her fever, her vomiting, when she showed him the buboes in her armpit and her groin, he shuddered. Peck's fingers were as slender and brittle as his cane which he rested on Lena's wrist. His voice was high and nasal. He did not touch her.

I will be leaving you this, said Peck holding a small scent box made of sandal wood before Lena. You must carry your scent box with you when you leave your bed. I prescribe an essence of rue, roses, cloves, and juniper; holding your scent box to your nose, inhale with every breath.

"Peck, Sir," said Licket. "May I have a word?"

The doctor nodded, his cap's bill nearly touching the blanket. Say what you will, Licket.

"In your misfortune, My Lady," said Licket, "try not to think of death. Nothing should distress you, direct your thoughts to pleasing, agreeable, and delicious things. Beautiful landscapes, fine gardens should be on your eyelids, particularly those with odoriferous plants. Let your imagination play beautiful, melodious songs. If you find the contemplation of gold and silver and precious stones a comfort to your heart, then by all means indulge yourself in such contemplations. My Lady, enjoy this fine season."

Come now, Licket, said Peck. Your eternal optimism is no comfort to this weary soul. Mrs. Romero, he means well. I would listen to him with waxed ear.

I shall, Doctor.

38

Now, I will nail a quarantine sign on your door
to protect those in Rio Barranca. You must remain
within for at least two weeks or until the buboes in
your groin subside. You have stocked up on
supplies? You will not starve here alone?

I have food. Licket will be my comfort.

"Yes, My Lady."

I must go now, said Peck.

Goodbye, Doctor. And, thank you.

The man lowered the canopy and left Lena to
herself. Licket, after a whistle from his master, went
a distance away and taking a running jump landed
firmly on Peck's shoulder. The two friends left
Lena's rooms together, presumably to recount old
memories.

Lena closed her eyes and breathed of the languid
aromas the doctor had left behind. Once before she
slept, she heard a hammering at her door, a pounding
that sounded like a shotgun's blasts, that startled
her from her sleep. A short while afterwards, she
felt Licket crawl under the canopy and curl at the
foot of her bed where Dr. Dee would have slept
were he present.

10. "We will do the bank of the Barranca,"

Purty Romero wasn't the prick teaser that some are, and she wasn't as hard as she might be. If her mother had let her run the least bit looser, chances are she would have twirled, herself, on the stools with the pin-curled, Saturday night whores at the Arsenal Bar on the outskirts of Rio Barranca. Even though Purty wasn't ever too concerned who it was that fucked her, her flesh was still soft.

She was a perfect mark for Digger Monatti, and Digger liked women who had saved a little softness somewhere along the trail. She held off visiting Irma Slate's grave as long as she could. When she did go, she went solemn carrying flowers.

"Were you very close," he asked her.

"Oh! You startled me. Mr. Monatti, I am Purty Romero, an old student of Miss Slate's."

"I know," said Digger.

And, they carried on a conversation.

Digger Monatti's father was killed over near the

Arizona border when an acid truck he was driving lost its brakes. "That was nine years ago," he said. "You can still see where the sulphuric ate into the limestone. Maybe you would care to go over there with me sometime. I put a brass marker on the guard rail."

"I think I would like that," said Purty. "To go with you to visit the place your father died, I mean."

"The tire marks are gone now. At one time you could see just where the skid started and where the back tires began to whip before the truck tank slapped the rock wall. There have been a lot of accidents on that road, but my old man had the worse one ever. They say that when the lid blew on the tank, acid shot a hundred feet up the wall and fell back onto the truck like a geyser. Burned to a crisp by fire and acid."

"How old were you?" asked Purty, her eyes moist.

"I was seventeen at the time. They showed me the pictures the highway patrol took."

"My mother," said Purty, "is called Bicycle Lena. She suffers from delusions and has not spoken to me for more than two years."

"No one is certain who my mother was," said Digger. "From the looks of me she was an Indian." Digger smoothed his hair back with his fingers. "I come originally from Gallup. So that's probably true."

Purty stooped to arrange the flowers she was carrying. As she rested a coffee can on the fresh grave, the wind filled her hair and billowed her light blue dress. She looked into the distance out over Rio Barranca to the horizon.

"Digger Monatti," she said, "I am glad that you are here. It is a comfort to have a gentleman in this town." She looked up at him all the while fondling a medallion hanging low around her neck. She reacted unconsciously to the man. Almost without realizing it, she found herself standing next to him very close. "When we are alone like this," she breathed, "may I call you Lou?"

It was with great difficulty that she stopped herself from taking Digger's hand and leading him down to her special place on the grassy bank of the Barranca river that first afternoon.

11. The Lady from Phoenix.

Licket did not seem to disturb Lena Romero, who
slept covered with a dark blanket, when he slipped
under the canopy and curled at the foot of her bed.
Perspiration ran off the woman's forehead, her upper
lip, and the folds in her neck. Her arms lay outside
the blanket at her sides. Aside from her lips, the
only other part of her that moved was her feet,
crossed at the ankle, they jerked involuntarily.

To quiet her, Licket began to whisper. "You told
them. You warned them about everything you saw.
The gas. The tremors. You did all you could, My
Lady. Now, try to sleep."

Lena smiled. I warned them that they were killing
themselves and only one person listened. No human
ears could hear Lena Romero's words.

At the far end of the room, she had strung a
clothes line. The line hung with black washing
except for a yellow towel. Lena could find no one
who sold black towels. An open box of dried cereal,

a carton of powdered milk, and a jar of open jam were on the table.

The Lovely Lady from Phoenix.

A bell sounded far away. An ice-cream man's bell maybe. A bicycle bell. A cash register.

How has the business been?

About thirty so far. Ingrid Bloomstrom. Lena employed one full-time clerk, Ingrid Bloomstrom, an attractive Swedish girl, who had almost super-human talents for running the Road Runner Shop. She could handle customers, sell overstock with ease, and unload delivery vans. The drivers who came in and out of Rio Barranca lived to see Ingrid in her leather apron lifting boxes. As Ingrid acquired more skill at managing the shop, Lena could spend less time there herself. She was grateful for Ingrid's skill, and she did little more than poke her head in the door some days.

About thirty so far, Ingrid Bloomstrom answered. A couple of peyote hatchets, a small rug, peasant blouse, one of Ernie Hinkle's bracelets.

"That's good, don't you think," said Licket.

Again, Lena Romero spoke but could not be heard by human ears. The Lady listened, she insisted she be told.

Licket said, "She was riding in a very old, shiny, black car. Chauffeured."

I was wearing my red dress, velvet. A crimson scarf.

"Purty was with you in her carriage."

I talked to them and she was the only one to listen.

"You stood proud on the corner quietly rocking Purty while you spoke to them."

She was so beautiful.

Lena sputtered. Her eyes opened and closed quickly, her fists clenched white against the blanket. She did not look grotesque, the flutter and rolling of her eyes was a nervous reflex, more melodrama than madness.

"They passed by you. And you stood and spoke magnificent."

"The Lady from Phoenix said to you, 'And, with such a beautiful child. They pity you, My Dear. Come to me.' "

"Yes," said Licket. "The Lovely Lady said, 'What is that child's name?' Next to her on the leather seat was a swan. Black."

She wore over her bronzed body a blouse, a squaw dress that reached her ankle and split up along her thigh. She opened the door for me.

"You moved quickly to sit next to her."

My heart was racing. My legs had melted. I could not stop myself from the warm press of her thigh against mine as she spoke to me.

"The Lady said, 'You are a proud woman. And, you have a very beautiful child.' Her voice was low and strong, 'I will name my swan Purity.' She reached to close the curtains on the windows of the car."

And sitting close to me she listened about the fumes, and the upheaval, the poison air, the warnings in the sky. Yes. She listened and told me one day I would receive a blessing.

"The Lady said, 'Would you like to touch me.' She opened her blouse and offered you her naked breast."

Against her smooth tanned skin there had been cut a cross, a scarred cross that raised white against her tan.

" 'Bring the child close to me.' She held your daughter against the cross."

She ran her hand behind my neck, she pulled me down to her.

" 'Kiss me if you wish, My Dear.' "

"And, she began to kiss you. She ran her hands over you."

Oh. The Lady from Phoenix. She gave me her blessing. She held her hands against me, she breathed into my mouth. She opened my dress and caressed me so gently. She passed to me a cross.

Lena's hands were relaxed. She had placed them on her breast before falling into a deeper, peaceful sleep. She did not hear Licket tell her he was going outside for a while, she did not feel him slide out from under the canopy. "I will be home before dark," said Licket. "I am going to the reservoir to chase sticks."

Chapter three.

12. "if I can call you Lou."

Purty chose the spot where she used to come with
Lou Willis, when she led Digger down to the
Barranca river for their first time. Nearly everyone
in town knew how Lou and Purty would meet by
Pfizer Lawrence's and walk down the steep path by
his laboratory to the river bank. A number could
point to the exact spot.

And was Lou something. Lord! He just had to
touch her and she would melt. In fact, in the
beginning it had actually shamed her, his melting
touch. Then, the times at the river came to feel so
natural that she wanted to go on for ever. Her times
with Lou became closer to life than anything she
could imagine. She felt awkward when she did anything else. Being with Lou on the banks of the
Barranca river came like breathing. Why, just the
thought of Lou sent her off.

Before the sex became obvious, Lena Romero was
pleased at her daughter's prospects and talked about

the couple with the neighbors. Then Purty made Lena into a fool.

One night, when she came home long after sunset, exhausted, tousled, smelling fresh of sex, her dress stained and wrinkled, and threw herself spread legged in a chair saying, "Oh, Mama. I sure love that man," Lena saw what had been going on between them and she went a little crazy. She jumped at Purty and began slashing at her clothes and skin calling her a whore. She locked herself in her apartment for close to ten days, and when she came back out onto the street, she simply was not the same person. Most everyone in town called her Bicycle Lena after that.

Purty fled the house, her coarse black hair loose, her dress in shreds, her eyes red and rimmed with mascara. She married Lou fast and they lived in the hotel for a week before he came out to go north looking for work. Two days later the troopers found his car smashed on the Red Mesa road. There was a woman in there with him, and Purty never forgave Lou that.

Though Purty let her sex go to sleep for a while, she never did go home. In time, the wildness in her returned. Her memories of Lou were strong. Sometimes she would go half crazy in her room alone aching for those same feelings again. Purty was simply wild by nature, and Lou Willis had done no more than show her what wild people liked and how they went about getting it.

Digger brought a rubberized Army poncho with them when Purty led him down to the Barranca river for their first time. She lay down on the poncho and stretched. She took a beer from Digger and shook her hair loose. She flipped off her shoes, and she stretched to her toes. Her thighs were open and strong against her velvet pants. Her breasts set firm. The beer moistened her lips. When Digger took her hand, she reached for the back of his neck. Her nails were long. She ran one along his scar. She nibbled his lip. Digger had hit her fast. His touch whipped up the old thick dizziness, and with him she didn't have to moan and breathe heavy to get herself started. Before he had her blouse off, her thighs were working on the hot, slippery rubber. He worked on her for a while, then she worked on him.

"We had better come down here as much as we can before the river goes down and starts to smell," said Purty clinging to his arm on the way up the steep path from the bank of the Barranca river with Digger Monatti after their first time.

nice touch

51

13. Johnny Ouranous.

The Geiger-Muller tube is a device filled with a rarefied gas which becomes electrically charged by the radioactive alpha particles in elements such as uranium and radium that are thrown off during the element's spontaneous disintegration. The Geiger counter is a device designed to record and measure the intensity of the element's disintegration in various areas of radioactivity. This decaying can be heard in the form of static emitted from the Geiger counter's amplifier or seen on a dial. When radioactivity is high in an area, the instrument sounds a continuous, rapid series of clicks. All radioactive phenomena decay completely in time, and the ultimate end product is one of the isotopes of lead. Half-decay period is the way decay time is measured. While some radioactive substances have half-lives of a fraction of a second, others have half-lives of a vast number of years.

The old prospectors and pocket hunters always had a weathered look about them, a worn but permanent look like Indian sandstone. Ragged from weeks of dry camping, scrambling in the rocks, living out of nothing more than a bean pot, their memories focused on their burros, their dead burros, their lost burros, the tired old burro, still standing, tied to a railing.

Johnny Ouranous was just as beat up, weathered down, and worn out by the country as any old-time, hard-rock prospector. His face didn't look so much like Indian sandstone as it did paste, he had a neon tan. Johnny Ouranous had come to Rio Barranca during the uranium boom in the fifties, the frenzied, electrified, uranium rush that burned many a strong, young man down and held him there until he broke, baffled by the ruthless finality of the Geiger counter he carried with him and crazed by the endless race to sweep and stake the most ground.

Johnny's boots were turquoise and polished, his hat was blocked with no sign of stain, his snap-button shirt and gabardine pants, pressed. He had never owned a burro, but he loved his four-wheel drive jeep as much as any old-timer loved his burro, and his Geiger counter as much as any loved his pan. The whites of Johnny O's cobalt eyes were discolored. He could see all right, but he wasn't supposed to drive directly into the sun. Johnny had burned part of his life looking for gold, "Set Taylor Basin to the north. Climb Dead Indian Draw . . . ."

But it was the uranium hunting that burned him down the most.

Johnny now worked at Lupine's Bar and Grill. When it wasn't busy he sat in the semi-darkness of the Bar looking into a glass of beer. Lupine didn't mind if he drank beer out front when it was slack, but she allowed him no hard stuff until five sharp.

When he poured a shot, he could measure it by sound and he never spilled a drop. He turned the full shot glass before him, tilted back his hat, bent his right arm and tossed the contents way in the back of his mouth. He slammed the glass down and simultaneously stomped his right foot on the bar rail causing his spurs to nick the stool rung and set up a ringing spin that lasted a long while after the pop of the shot glass hitting the bar. Pulling on his hat rim, he returned to his former position facing the bar, forearms on the edge, looking into the beer. "Set Taylor Basin to the north. Climb Dead Indian Draw up to Greasy Creek. Five hundred yards northwest." Johnny Ouranous went through nearly a case of whiskey every twenty-four days. Some set their watches when Johnny O. reached behind the bar for his bottle.

14. Night life.

"Hey, Lupine honey," said Chuck Swanson as he
leaned into the kitchen his hat in his hand. "Let me
buy you a snort."

"Go on with you, Chuck Swanson," said Lupine.

A cat slept curled in the corner, a half empty bowl
of milk nearby.

"Isn't that Bicycle Lena's cat?"

"Sure is. He's as crazy as Lena. When she starts
to go strange, he always come running to me.
Knows when to go back home too. Don't bother me
none, I got plenty here to feed him."

Chuck walked into the bar. Johnny Ouranous sat
over a whiskey at the far end near the window. The
neon sign flashing set his face apart from the green
shirt and light brown hat he was wearing. Johnny O.
moved his mouth rubbing his lips together. "Set
Taylor Basin to the north. Climb Dead Indian Draw
up to Greasy Creek. Five hundred yards northwest."

His voice was barely audible, he kept his eyes down.

Sometimes a man tended bar, others people helped themselves. "Pour your own and keep track of the tab." The place to an outsider was about as friendly as a VFW. If a group was large, Lupine asked them to buy a bottle. She gave set-ups free.

Digger Monatti sat at the opposite end of the bar alone. Chuck opened a beer and joined him.

"The name's Monatti. Digger Monatti. How are you going?"

"About half," he said shaking Digger's hand. "Chuck Swanson here."

"Sit yourself," said Digger.

Chuck Swanson said: "Why, I was driving out on County Route Nine yesterday after that rain we had and came up to that series of arroyos where the road dips and curves. If you do more than twenty-five, you will shake your truck to pieces. I noticed a huge bank of thunderheads moving in from the north. It was still raining like hell up there. Like a son of a bitch. The rumbling began just as I came to that big steel bridge. You have to wind down to it, shaking and shimmying to beat all hell on the washboard. Now, I have heard rumblings, flood rumblings, all my life, but never rumblings as big as these. This was like boulders crashing together in a concrete ditch. Now, that bridge is made of plate steel on top and fifteen inch beams underneath, and I have seen water six, ten inches over the top of it. Well, I was half way down and there she came. A wall of water more than twenty feet high the color of red clay. You never saw anything like it. Logs, stumps, sage, I even saw old car bodies, all swirling up front. And, when it hit that steel bridge, look out. It bent like a wet pretzel. I figure that's the biggest flash flood I have ever seen. Missed me by ten feet, a short ten feet. Why, if I hadn't been creeping down that washboard, it would have picked me up, truck and all, and carried me clean to the border."

"Whee. That's close," said Digger reaching over the bar for another beer.

Digger said: "Back in San Francisco, they were using plexi-glass bubbles on the coffins for a while. Well, at the services, they toss in a little dirt and leave the rest of the filling for the attendants."

Purty Romero slid onto the bar stool next to Digger. "Hello, Rosebud." When Digger smiled, his scar curled in a near-spiral around the corner of his mouth making his mustache look more barren than before. "Now, you sit quiet there while I speak with Mr. Swanson. Then, how about us going off some-place." Purty settled herself onto the soft plastic stool and smiled. When she put her hand on Digger's thigh, he flinched.

"The grave man does the real filling. At some of your bigger places they use payloaders. I heard of a few cases of rock falling on the plexi-glass. That kind of thing. Well, I used to fill by hand, and one day I was going down the line with two or three left before quitting time when I looked down into this hole. There was an old man looking right back at me. He was looking up and I know damn well he could see. His mouth was frozen in a scream and his hands were slowly pounding on the glass and he was kicking his feet like he was moving in clear jelly. He had one of those big rings on, and he must have been beating for quite a while because there was a section about as big as your head all scratched up right near his hand. Hell, you can bet I started filling like mad. From the head down."

"Wheew," said Chuck.

"Morbid," said Digger. "Well, let's go, Rosebud."

"Nice talking to you," said Chuck.

"Yea, Chuck," said Digger.

15. Ya-hoo!

Digger smiled as he closed the car door his shoes
crackling on the gravel drive. Purty had the African
drum music going. When he looked in the cottage
window he saw her head thrown back eyes closed
caressing herself as she moved with abandon to the
music.

She cupped her breasts and swayed toward the
door moving her pelvis, she wore a short nightgown
with orange and black fur tufts on the sleeves neck
and hem. Digger opened the door and held up the
whiskey bottle.

"How did you know it was me?"

"I didn't," she said her eyes still closed.

"Ya-hoo!" he said popping snaps on his cowboy
shirt.

16. After the third edaphic fuse.

While in the city, it had been Robert Quinn's habit to keep a commentary or log of his activities. He used the past tense, third person. The commentary, quite naturally, was always a few hours behind his true actions.

The people who searched his apartment, the landlady and a police officer, found Quinn's log on the kitchen table and were the first to read the log's last entry. It seems that he had had a full day, and he had gone a number of places. Quinn begins the entry by saying:

"Katie was being very patient. She had fed the cat his milk and was sitting across the room reading *Earth* while Quinn caught up here. [Note: *Earth* is a fine ecological paper, he hopes to write an article for them one day.]"

The formal section of that day's entry begins as the entries usually did with Quinn getting out of bed and shaving. He had put in a new blade that morning.

The landlady and the police officer skipped to the end of the entry. They began to read seriously at the point where Katie and Quinn were crossing Seventh Avenue along Tenth Street:

"The light was green but the bulb was burned out, so they could not tell for certain whether to walk or not. He was thinking about the half gallon of milk tucked under his arm and how it would change the color of the evening if they were hit by a truck. A few other people were standing on the curb and they all looked up the street. One man said, 'Hell, I'm going.' He walked safely across. The others left the curb after the man and also made it safely across. Quinn had a premonition that the light was going to change. He couldn't deny that. But he started to cross anyway. As they raised their left feet, Katie and Quinn always walked in step, as they stepped off the curb, he looked up the street and saw a huge truck coming right at them. . . ."

Robert's journal stopped at that point.

"Those poor kids," said the landlady as she locked the door to Robert Quinn's apartment with her pass key.

"I hope they made it," said the police officer tipping his hat to the landlady before continuing his patrol.

II.

Chapter four.

17. Happy Dan gets kicked upstairs.

Remember Happy Dan Anderson, the colorful cardboard cutout she carted around with her and set up
when she needed a bar companion to make herself
legitimate, the vague, distracted man who enjoyed
two things, breeding Siamese cats and cracking his
bull whip. Old Happy Dan, he was sure happy when
he was standing in the center of the highway with
his cats cracking his whip. And, when he cracked
that whip, the echo would peel off the foothills just
like the blast of a high-powered rifle.

Well, Happy Dan has got kicked upstairs. There
he was in uniform, bush hat, white coat, boots,
standing in the road in front of the snake museum
when it happened.

The lights of the car stopped him like a strobe
with his arm back. As he was propelling the whip
forward for a crack, the car got him. At least, the
driver claims he heard a crack a split second before
he struck something in the road.

Happy Dan Anderson, arm reared, whip cracking, cats at his feet, was propelled into the darkness by a speeding vehicle on County Route Nine.

If the driver of the speeding car didn't think about Happy Dan being absent, he could remember seeing him with his back to the car, a crack uncoiling from the bull whip in such a fashion that he was drawn behind the straightening whip like an escaped billboard illustration and pulled out of sight.

The driver swore there had been cats at Happy Dan's feet, but they were gone too when he got out to see if he could locate what he had hit.

So long Happy Dan!

18. Desperate dreams.

The girls were like dreams. Pfizer Lawrence watched
them swimming in the Barranca river. He watched
them, hair wild in the wind, walk the path by his
laboratory, down the switch-backs, to the river. The
girls wore soft blouses. They were remote, even the
most liberated corners of Pfizer's youth didn't hold
such sights.

Two figures appeared far down the road. Pfizer
saw them from his laboratory window as they
approached, walking slowly, almost floating. He
recognized them from silhouette, Cornelia, the tall
blonde, and Sergia, the brunette. Both girls were
fourteen, but they could make themselves seem very
much older.

"Babies are perfect," said Cornelia, "if you don't let
them grow up with a lot of garbage in their heads."

"They can be total love," said Sergia. "If
you don't teach them that certain things are

wrong or dirty, they will have pure minds."

They both were silent, walking. Then Sergia said, "It is right about the karma cycle. The cause and effect do spiral. When I am afraid, my fear will spiral on itself."

"We can deny fear," said Cornelia, "that will break the spiral."

Pfizer hurried from his laboratory through the front parlor and out the door onto the porch where he sat in the swing, his anticipation hidden with a magazine. He hoped they would stop and talk with him before going down the path. He knew he wouldn't know what to say. As the girls walked toward Pfizer, floating, slowly, they came close enough to recognize him. He lowered his magazine, and he saw them wave at him. Pfizer smiled and fluttered the magazine.

"I believe in chemistry," said Cornelia.

The girls passed the laboratory and began the steep descent to the Barranca river.

"It is quiet," said Sergia.

"It makes you realize how old the town really is," said Cornelia.

"It feels abandoned."

"Pompeii."

From a distance they seemed to float down the path. The slow motion of the wind in their long hair lifted them. The swaying of their walk made their dresses caress them. They looked as though their feet did not touch the ground as they walked down the steep path to the river for a swim.

19. *Datura* (one).

Indian Charlie and Ernie Hinkle drove into Rio Barranca. Indian Charlie, cross-legged, rode in the back. He had come to town with Ernie to sell a few postcards. Wrapping himself in his blanket, he squatted on the sidewalk in front of Lena Romero's Road Runner Shop. Placing his pottery bowl on his right, he fanned the postcards in front of him, and he smiled. When Ernie rushed out of the Shop a few minutes later, he was blushing and seemed quite agitated.

Ingrid Bloomstrom, Lena Romero's assistant, gave a tight scream when she stepped out of the bathroom and saw a pair of men's trousers behind the dress rack. However, she seemed delighted and actually became quite animated when she saw that the trousers belonged to a man with red rims around his eyes and large ears who she knew was no stranger at all but Mr. Hinkle, the Meticulous Handmade Indian Jewelry Man.

"Why, hello, Mr. Hinkle."

"Hello, Ingrid. You really should call me Ernie," he said. He saw how her blue eyes flashed, how her body seemed full, her long blonde hair glistening as it hung loose and grainy against her soft brown face and neck.

"Ernie, I didn't see you come in," she said.

"I hope I didn't startle you." He liked her breasts and sweet face. She was pretty and fresh in the light blue skirt and blouse she was wearing.

"Oh. I scream a lot," she said.

As he made notes on little white cards, he found himself watching her across the store. Her clothes seemed so thin as she moved that he swore he could see her body beneath them.

"Ingrid," he said a few moments later. "Will Lena be ordering more jewelry soon? I have some new designs that should be ready in a few weeks." He found it much easier to approach Ingrid without Lena Romero there watching.

"Oh. You will. But, Lena has gone away again. She told me to buy nothing more until her illness has passed." Ingrid looked sad.

"Oh. And, you are left here to run the shop alone."

"But, your beautiful jewelry, who will buy it?"

"Someone will," he said. "And, I hope you might like to come and see the new things I have made sometime."

"Yes," she said. "But, I hope you will let me try some on, Ernie." She walked to him and stood closer

than she ever had before. "You must promise to give
me fair warning, I must lie in the sun before coming.
I look very much like an Indian when I wear
turquoise and have a little sunburn. Very much like
an Indian when I am dripping with turquoise." She
put her hand on his arm. "Promise?"

Ernie was blushing when he rushed out of the Road
Runner Shop a few minutes later and climbed in the
truck. Indian Charlie, having sold a few cards, was
sitting in the back eating a candy bar.

20. Katie.

On Pelado hill north of Rio Barranca near the
reservoir, Robert Quinn, a recent copy of *Earth* in
his hand, sat on the front steps of the Mud Rocket
looking off down the hill toward the valley of the
Barranca river. Cornelia was sunning herself nearby.

"Here comes Katie," she said pointing toward a
grove of cottonwood trees down the hill.

Quinn said, "She walks in the woods like a spirit.
She doesn't seem afraid. She takes me in the woods
that way forgetting I am there."

Katie in a white muslin dress was walking toward
them. He watched her drift up the trail, her dress
·turning leaves, brushing against the grass, her legs
and feet unseen. He watched her taking quick steps
which he knew hardly made a sound.

"She is trying to teach me softness. With flowers,
she bends down to them. She opens her fingers and
handles the stems gently while she looks at them.
She nestles the flower's heads, which never does

73

more than flick away the dew. She always lets them free again. She is trying to teach me softness by the way she is with flowers.

"If deer are grazing in a field, she will spend hours waiting for them to finish. She has no urge to frighten them. She is trying to teach me softness and she wants to eliminate the shotgun that blasts in my brain from habit each time I flush a pheasant in a field for when we are walking and she hears that noise it disturbs her."

"She will one day," said Cornelia as Quinn touched her cheek and walked down the path. He waved with his copy of *Earth*, Katie returned the wave with her hand.

21. The gift.

The watch Johnny Ouranous wore on his drinking arm had once been part of a display in the window of Chuck Swanson's hardware store. For nearly two years, the watch, attached to a leather band which was in turn attached to an armature driven by a small electric motor, was dipped into a plastic dish filled with water, lifted out, smashed against an anvil-shaped magnet, and held motionless for a moment, so the spectator could see that it continued to run, before the electric mechanism sent it on its cycle once again.

When Chuck first got the watch display from the manufacturer, he changed the water in the plastic dish regularly. As time went by, more pressing matters took over, and fungus began to grow along the sides of the dish. Still, the watch was self-winding, and the display worked quietly day and night in the corner of Swanson's front window. When the water had evaporated and the fungus had turned brown, the little motor still worked and the armature continued to guide the watch through its cycle. When the watch had worn away the thin, magnetic coating on the anvil and had begun to dig into the plaster base beneath, the watch, its face white with plaster dust, continued to tick.

One morning, Johnny Ouranous, as usual, was passing by the hardware store on his way to Lupine's, and he noticed that the leather strap had broken and that the ticking watch had fallen into the bed of brown fungus. He saw that the weightless armature was flailing erratically causing the entire display card to vibrate and actually edge toward the sun glass display close by.

Johnny interrupted his walk to Lupine's long enough to find the plug, save the sun glasses, and receive the watch as a gift from Chuck Swanson. Johnny bought an expandable band from Chuck and proudly put the watch on his drinking arm.

Chapter five.

22. "He was stepping out on me, Sheriff,"

"They found Wild Chico Mendez this morning," said Martin Walters. "Drunk or doped up, he missed the bridge. Cracked his skull open."

"Does he go in at the cemetery?" asked Digger Monatti.

"No, the Chicano yard by the river."

Except for a few red neon lights and the rest room signs, all but the most prominent details in the Arsenal Bar were continually in obscurity. Even the floor man did his work in half light. The room was square, the bar itself formed a smaller square, its far side against the wall. The entrance, a thick wood door, was directly in front of the building. The windows had been bricked over, and the walls were thick enough to seal out the trunk noise and hold the music in.

Four or five people were scattered around the room aside from Martin, Digger, and Estelle Anderson sitting in a booth. Estelle wore a dress cut low enough to show the snake's head when she leaned across the table to talk.

"I might like to dig his hole," said Monatti. He looked direct and hard at Estelle. "Sometimes you have some pretty interesting thoughts digging a grave for a man who had a violent death." Digger's scar glistened, he swung his stare over to Martin. "I have this feeling, Martin, I would think about you."

"Now, that's mighty neighborly," said Martin. "Don't you think so, Estelle."

"Boys," said Estelle leaning way out on the table to look at both of them at once.

"If you want to dig Mendez's grave so bad, I am sure someone in the family will be glad to hand you the shovel." Martin put his arm around Estelle and pulled her to him. His belly pushed against his silver belt buckle. "Monatti, it may come close." Martin's voice was slow. "But, I'm not dying here as long as you are doing the burying."

"You got to be a mighty powerful man to control that," Digger smiled.

"You got to be strong. Especially when you have the breath of a grave digger going down your neck. Right, Estelle?"

Digger had been in lots of fights, and he didn't mind them. Martin hadn't used his fists for a long while and was quick to submit if he lost no ground. He pulled Estelle up closer to him and kissed her on the cheek.

"I'm getting us some more to drink," said Martin looking to the bar. "Same all around?"

Digger and Estelle nodded.

"Hands away, Mister," said Estelle. "Don't touch
the merchandise unless the lady asks. And," she
soothed, "if she does ask, handle her gentle."

"Your husband know you are here, Little Lady,"
asked Digger.

"My husband is no longer with me."

"Who takes care of you now?"

"Nobody in particular."

Martin passed around the drinks. Digger gave him a
quarter for the juke box. Estelle took off her shoe
and slowly played her warm foot against Digger.
When Martin sat back down, she moved close to
him and held hands in his lap. If there had been a
few more people around, more than likely there
would have been a fight.

23. Quinn's article for *Earth*

*At present there are almost two thousand of my
geodesic domes in forty countries around the world.
All of those structures are of an unprecedented
type. They were patentable in the countries around
the world because they were unprecedented and
were not included in structural engineering theory
and therefore were true inventions. They enclose
environments at about one percent of the invested
weight of resources of comparable volume enclosed
by conventional structures with which you are
familiar. They had to meet the hurricanes, the snow
loads, and so forth. My structures are also earth-
quake proof; most of their comparable conventional
counterparts are not. I have found it possible to do
much more with less. (R. Buckminister Fuller, 1962)*

It isn't as difficult as some of you may think to
build your own dome in the middle of the wilder-
ness. Here we are in Rio Barranca! We did it without

any previous knowledge and have already graduated from our VW camper (more about that in a minute) to our majestic adobe house with a dome. And we built it all ourselves. In fact, I am now in the dome room, writing this article by kerosene lamp.

The Indians settled this land first. Pueblo Indians, they raised corn and tried to live in peace. Pueblo Barranca itself has been inhabited continuously for more than nine hundred years, now the only thing left is a trading post and a few run-down adobe buildings where the remaining fifty-seven members of the tribe make stone, clay, and glass ware for the tourists.

Things started going down hill for the Indians in 1670 when a detachment of Coronado's exploratory force, who supposedly came up the river's gorge looking for gold, discovered the Indian's pueblo high above them and scaled the ravine's walls to see what they could see. The Spaniards were taken by the peaceful way of life and decided to settle there too.

Probably they found the steep path from the river to the Indian's dwelling a rough climb and that was the reason they named the river *El Rio Barranca de los Cojos,* which roughly translates into "The River Gorge of Lame Men." The town of Rio Barranca still sits on the lip of the gorge a mile north of the old Indian pueblo. The river meanders a lot more than it did in 1670, and today there are a number of paths leading down to the grassy river bank.

The country to the south of us is dry scrub brush, desert plateaus. To the north are the woods and mountains. We live a good distance from town, between the desert and the peaks, near cottonwood trees, near sheer sandstone walls, not far from Alameda creek which runs into the Barranca river, on Pelado hill. Geologists say our hill is surrounded by a metamorphic aureole. I think that is terrific. The sunsets over Red Mesa off to the far west are absolutely breath-taking—cumulus shattered with sunlight to bursting. It is very great to breathe, work, and live on a nimbus of metamorphic aureole. It's idyllic here!

How did we get to Rio Barranca? The usual story. Luck. I was living in the city and going through the hassle, the muggings, the rapes, the murders, the traffic. Why talk about it. The bad air, the rotten food, the dog shit, the taxi drivers.

I was sitting in my apartment, and a friend called to say he had inherited one thousand acres in Rio Barranca. He is in electro-physics and can't use the land for a few years. Did I want to use it? That's the first part of the luck. Then more followed. I met Katie who wanted to go with me. We found a camper and left. Just like that. Split.

Let me quickly say here. It may seem natural to put the kitchen in the rear compartment above the engine box. Okay. But not in winter. Kate nearly froze her ass off standing out there trying to cook supper. The camper was full of stuff and it took us one entire afternoon to rebuild a kitchen inside. We insulated with cardboard, carpets, and some quilts.

84

We arrived in Rio Barranca in late March. There were two girls, Cornelia and Sergia, squatting on the land living in a teepee. Katie and I stayed in the camper, and the four of us ate together. I built a sort of shed you could park the camper against, and Katie cooked in there on an old wood stove.

As soon as the ground thawed, we began to make adobe bricks. In no time, we had the Mud Rocket. It was supposed to be a simple one-story building with a flat roof, but we couldn't patch the leaks, so we capped it with a dome of silver metal and light crushed rock. The Mud Rocket! You should see it as you wind up Pelado hill, it's like Palomar. Spectacular!

We haven't any electricity or plumbing yet, and we have to carry water from Alameda creek, but it outpaces any dwelling in any city I have ever seen.

I am thinking about raising chickens and a few pigs. You must have heard about those digestors that use the gas from decomposing pig shit to operate a generator. A coil of copper tubing spiraled into the digestor and filled with circulating, heated water is supposed to increase the efficiency a good deal. We run on kerosene now because, until we get some animals, we don't generate enough garbage to keep a digestor going. I am also going to build a shed soon. Once you start on this building trip, it's impossible to stop.

But, there's no hurry. Life goes on steady and

slow out here. The sun doesn't rise onto a pile of gold nuggets like they used to say, but it is mighty damn nice. You really ought to try doing it yourself sometime.

24. The dowser.

Martin Walters had an office in his snake museum.
It was a long office with two windows at either end.
On one wall, traps, guns, gold pans, railroad spikes,
Indian headdresses, and newspaper clippings about
hangings, hunting, floods, the uranium rush and
bomb shelters. On the other, the overflow from the
relic corner, costumes Jenny wore, her hook, and a
series of posters, carnival posters, illustrating buxom
Izella the Snake Lady, a woman who could beguile
the most deadly, seduce the most powerful, and
overwhelm the most enticing. To a spectator,
Martin's life seemed to be filled with memorabilia
of his dead wife.

Martin sat with his feet on the window ledge
looking through the Venetian blind onto the highway. He was dressed for Fiesta, boots, pressed
snap shirt, string tie, hat with no sweat stain,
dress pants, a wide hand-tooled belt with a huge
silver and turquoise buckle. He looked dignified,

but slightly corrupt, like a successful oil man.

As Pfizer opened the door, Martin began a slow turn in his chair. "Thanks for coming by Pfizer," he said without looking up. "I watched you crossing the gravel. I say, you have more curiosity than a pissing dog. It's a wonder you ever get where you are going."

"Nothing of it," said the chemist walking to the posters. He examined them all carefully.

"She was quite a woman, I bet," said Pfizer.

"Why, Jenny could get one of them constrictors to make three sometimes four turns, they never bruised a bone. She could charm a sidewinder around her little finger. Hell, she charmed me. No doubt about that. No doubt at all. Well, let's get to it. Got a problem, Pfizer. Best get at it."

"Shoot," said Pfizer.

"Want to drill me a well."

"Need a rig?"

"Nope. A dowse."

"A dowse."

"Yup. Where do I get one?"

"Swanson been talking to you?"

"Maybe."

"Sure, I know a few."

"Who?"

"There are a couple near Albuquerque. Hard to find though."

"Well, who then?"

"Indian Charlie?"

Indian Charlie smelled like a candle. He lived poor
from selling a picture postcard featuring himself at
Pueblo Barranca finishing a sand painting. Wrapped
in a blanket, a pottery bowl for change next to him,
he sat in front of Lena Romero's Road Runner
Shop smiling up at the tourists holding the postcards
like a fan.

"Indian Artisan at Work," the caption read. And
visitors to Rio Barranca bought a lot of Indian
Charlie's postcards. They liked his eager face smiling
out at them, they were delighted that Indian Charlie
had stopped working on his bright ceremonial design
long enough to have his picture taken. Though
Indian Charlie lived poor, he sold enough cards
during the season to make it through the winter and
early spring and still have enough money left over
to pay for a new order when the card salesman
made his swing through Rio Barranca each year.

"Him?"
    "Yup."
    "Know anybody else?"
    "Not close."
    "Set it up for me then," said Martin.
    "So long."
    "Thanks for coming by."
    "Nothing of it."

25. Curios.

Kachina dolls. Imports. Spanish styled furniture.
Squaw dresses. Film. Patio fashions. Prayer sticks.
Indian war bonnets. Ceramics. Portraits on velvet.
Coin purses.

The rack in the rear of Chuck Swanson's Hardware
was full of cartoon postcards, he had collected
hundreds of them and sold only duplicates. When
one of the magazines advertised a special mechanism
that would magnify an image many times, Swanson
sent away for it. On a large piece of wallboard he
reproduced his favorite.

The postcard girl looked to have experienced two
mishaps at virtually the same moment, the wind had
caught the hem of her skirt and tossed it to her low,
tight, sheer blouse and the elastic on her pink
panties had snapped. Since she had a hat and purse
in one hand and a large package in the other, the
girl could do little more than pose, her shiny

bottom thrust in full view. She was blushing, but had managed somehow to retain the pie-wedge twinkles in each eye.

Life-sized "Windy Days" hung over Chuck Swanson's desk. He would lean back in his chair, boots crossed, and admire her. He would, at those moments, think about one of two things, either how much more beautiful she was than Izella the Snake Lady or how he would one day do her on peg board for the stock room.

26. *Datura* (two).

"Now, Indian Charlie, I have known you for a long time and I think we are close friends," said Ernie Hinkle. "Isn't that right?"

"That's right, Ernie."

"Okay, then. I hear you know a little something about the way to get women."

"A little. What do you want to know."

"I want to know about the magic way to get women."

"Yes, I know a little about that." Indian Charlie leaned back in the folding aluminum chair. It was quiet in Ernie Hinkle's cement-block jewelry factory. Indian Charlie's voice, slightly thick from whiskey, reverberated gently in the room. "So, you want to use some medicine to get a woman. I do not know how a white girl would be with the medicine. But, I think you might find it a very satisfactory copulation. What woman do you think of?"

"Ingrid Bloomstrom at the Road Runner Shop."

"Ah, yes. It would be a very satisfactory copulation."

Indian Charlie said, "They say they use the medicine on the reservation. The Chicanos taught the medicine to the Navajos. I do not believe that.

"They say when some of the trading posts have rodeos and dances, those that know how to use it, especially at the circle dances, put this stuff on the girls. They say the girls become crazy and run after the men and are busy having intercourse all night. I do not know. I have not been to those dances.

"Cone Towards Water and *datura* are mind medicine. They use My Thumb, Laughing Medicine, and Crushed Down Sumac sometimes. I have heard of a man who gave *datura* to a woman at a circle dance. They say she took off her dress and put it on top of her head and went after the man and caught him. They say she was busy with him and a lot of other men all night.

"You can drop the medicine in a person's shoe or his shirt or give it by kissing. You can put a little in her food or put it on her body with your finger. They say, it takes very little, and she will be after your penis.

"Some use Red Base, Milk Plant or mix them. I can get *datura* which is very good for this sort of thing. They say it is better to take some *datura* and some Cone Towards Water and mix them. They say it is very successful coupling when you use *datura* and Cone Towards Water. This Ingrid Bloomstrom will be very interested if you give her the medicine."

"Thank you, Indian Charlie. I hope so."

"She is very pretty and a very full girl," said Indian Charlie.

"She makes my knees weak."

"If you are silent a moment," said Indian Charlie, "you will be able to imagine what Ingrid Bloomstrom will be like when you give her the medicine. It is not difficult, close your eyes."

Slipping the silver under her blouse she said the silvery coolness felt so good against her sunburned skin. She lifted her blouse and rubbed the silver on her skin. She took a huge silver and turquoise brooch and moved it over her skin and skirt. She put turquoise bracelets on her upper arm and when she held herself they caressed her skin. Turning quickly she admired the silver string of beads she pressed against her breast. Turning again naked she went to the safe for herself. Elaborate thunderbird necklaces tiaras beads. Naked she decorated her hair her arms her neck. She rubbed the silver against her breasts her belly her thighs. She slipped bracelets on her arms and ankles. She wound beads around her thighs her waist. She caressed herself with the jewelry ran beads gently between her legs. And from the safe she took a beautiful silver powder horn. She held the horn against her cheek and she licked it with her tongue. Her scent was heavy and her breath rich as she walked into the warm moonlight. Turquoise covered her the silver reflected like thousands of mirrors the moonlight back. She worked the horn quietly in silence and after a time it fell away next to her in the rust colored sand.

"You look displeased," said Indian Charlie.

"I am not happy with what I imagined," said Ernie.

"Now you understand the *datura.* You will not need it with Ingrid Bloomstrom. I have always carried with me some of the medicine in a silver box, but I have never opened the box. I will get you *datura* and will mix it with Cone Towards Water. It is a good thing for a man to carry it with him."

27. Quinn's hat.

A small blaze, gas forced from the embers, caught
and died. Quinn rose and stacked more cedar logs
on the glowing coals; he felt like a cowboy.

"We used to have these fires in front of lean-tos
when I was small," he said. "We would burn pine
and maple, and the fire would last most of the
night. Sometimes deer or raccoons would nose
around the camp in the early morning. The land is
much softer back there."

The air on Pelado hill was crisp and still, sparks
shot high into the open night. Quinn sat near the
fire pit which was surrounded with a patio of rust-
colored flagstone. The fire threw a light ring thirty
feet into the darkness. Beyond the dome of light,
the land was dark and still, the Mud Rocket stood
silent, a domed fortress.

Quinn's short cropped beard was almost copper in
the light. "The Indian Laborer," he said. Those
sitting around the fire, Cornelia, Sergia, Katie looked

at him. He had received a silent request from them. Quinn was going to tell a story.

"The flash flood had done enough damage to the bridge on County Route Nine to require a repair crew of twelve. The last laborer to be chosen for the crew was an Indian.

"The men began work early, before the sun slowed them down, and they quit around mid-afternoon when it was the hottest. The arroyo was dry, the red clay had begun to crack and peel. At ten, the Supervisor, who spent most of his time in the truck, halted the men for a break. When the water bag was passed to the Indian Laborer, he slopped some of the water on the ground before he took a mouthful himself.

" 'Hey, Indian. We don't have enough water to waste,' said the Supervisor.

"The Indian Laborer said nothing, and the men went back to work.

"At the next break, the Indian Laborer did the same thing. Splashing a swallow on the ground before taking one himself.

"The Supervisor grabbed the water bag from the Indian and yelled at him, 'Bring your own water, Indian, if you want to work on this crew.'

"The workmen seemed appeased. The water bag was not passed to the Indian again. No one asked him why he spilled some of the water on the ground. He probably didn't really know himself."

Quinn removed his broadbrimmed planter's hat and capped his knee with it.

"Where did you get your hat, Quinn," asked Sergia.

"At a J.C. Penney's in Akron, Ohio."

Cornelia who was sitting closest reached for it and put it on. "It's very nice," she said.

The flames reached high licking over the top of the logs when he crawled into his sleeping bag next to Katie. She was soft in the firelight, sitting cross-legged mending, and she smiled when he climbed into bed. "Thanks for the story, Robert," she said.

Chapter six.

28. Quinn goes trout fishing.

From above he could see the trout, many of them, feeding in Alameda creek. He walked out on the rocks which made natural stepping places to a huge natural pool, and he quickly tied on a small trout fly. After a series of false casts to reel out some line, he landed the fly perfectly to a rising trout.

After landing the trout, he cast again. While a second trout rose suspicious to inspect his fly, Katie who had been walking in a grove of cottonwoods nearby appeared at the edge of the pool. When she walked her body became light, free, almost floating. Her smile and her eyes were deep, and she beckoned him to come away.

He left the more cumbersome part of himself at the pool's edge to lure the feeding trout and followed away behind her along the deer path, into the woods, up stream.

29. Desperate dreams.

He was awakened by a pounding on his laboratory
door. Cornelia stood on the back steps, Sergia was
with her. "I am Cornelia," she said.

"I know," said Pfizer opening the door.

Sergia sat rigid her eyes fixed on something just
beyond the wall. He crossed the room and turned
his back toward them the gas jet hissed, glass
tinkled, steel rattled. The laboratory noises startled
Sergia. He came to her with a beaker of colored
liquid. Carefully, he put his hand behind her neck
and massaged her. She closed her eyes and seemed
to rest while Pfizer spoke gently to her. When she
seemed relaxed and aware of him, he held the
beaker of liquid before her. "Sergia, will you please
drink this." She nodded and Pfizer brought the
beaker to her lips. A few moments later, Sergia
opened her eyes and looked directly at him.

"Thank you, Pfizer," she said.

"You are welcome," said Pfizer. He carried her to the couch where she fell asleep.

Cornelia rested in a chair.

Pfizer heard her footsteps. He heard the toilet flush, the tissue spinning off the roll. He saw through a veil her body, her thighs, her light fingers as they turned the shower knob. Her feet were delicate, warm against the bathroom rug. She was soft against the towel.

In the morning, he found a note which they had left. Two smiling flowers saying, "I love you, Mr. Chemist!" Folding the note carefully, he placed it in a tiny wooden box.

30. The kootch.

Estelle took his head and buried his face between her breasts.

"Take a smell, Mister. And, don't touch the merchandise unless the lady asks you to."

"You're beautiful, Estelle."

Holding her dress closed, she walked to the far end of the house trailer and switched on the radio. She walked back toward him, her voice was husky and strong, her movements slow and, the way he liked them, writhing. "And, if she does ask, Mister, you had better hold on tight."

Estelle always did her dance against a pole, a snorting pole, that was two inches in diameter, stainless steel and firmly screwed to the ceiling and floor.

"You're beautiful, Estelle." He grabbed at her breasts.

"Touch me with your eyes." She rubbed the pole, she pretended it began to swell, she pretended she was amazed and pleased, and she spread her legs and began to move against it, caressing it with her hands and body and her tongue. She danced well, each time she seemed to have aroused herself to the point of vacant frenzy, she would work with herself all the more.

The music was really pounding in his ears when she finally slid out of her clothes.

Naked, her back turned, she spread her legs and began to caress herself, she dropped to her knees, she propelled herself into a state of high abandon and yelled wild at the end of the song.

She did not turn to him but rested while she captured the insinuations of the following song. Once she got its rhythm, she turned. And, he saw her.

"Estelle, you're beautiful," he said.

She stood before him and moved. The tattoo on her belly moved with her, its tongue flicked at her breasts when she moved them. She went down slowly on her back, the snake crawling on her belly, and she said, "Come down, Mister. You take care of me."

And, like mad, he began unbuttoning.

31. The dowse.

"I was born with the water magic," said Indian
Charlie. "The body and mind of a water magic man
can unite to enter the wood. When he passes over
water, the electricity begins and he will have no
control. A force many times stronger than his
strength overtakes him."

Indian Charlie scratched his head and guided his
hair behind his ears. "I was little when I found
myself with the magic. I was returning into the hills
with my family, we were living far to the south of
here. I walked behind, my brain quiet. The road was
hard and black, a white man's road. Without
warning, my heart arm, a string must have been tied
to my thumb, extended itself. The electricity over-
took me. I stopped, frightened, and, my voice
shaking, asked my father to help me. When he saw
me standing in the center of the road, my arm
hanging over the hard road like it did not belong to
me, he began to laugh and hug me. The electricity

passed to him, and to rid ourselves of it we rolled together on the ground. That is when I realized I had the water magic.

"So, my friend," he continued. "There is no trick. The water magic is a gift."

Off to the east, Quinn's Mud Rocket. Below that, the Rio Barranca reservoir. The sky was cobalt blue, the horizon to the south over the town was so far away one could not see where earth and sky met. The Barranca river cutting through the strata sinuated green.

"Hello, Indian," said Martin Walters walking toward the men, "I hope the water spirits are on your side today."

"How do you do," said Indian Charlie. "My fee is two hundred and fifty for the initial search, and another two hundred and fifty if the drilling reaches the water."

"Hell," said Martin, "I've spent near that on the tests alone. You ever had well water, Pfizer. Five hundred don't begin to pay for that taste."

"I ask for the initial search fee as a cash advance, if you don't object."

"Object, hell. You just find me a nice bunch of water right down there." Martin pointed along the edge of the drive toward his ranch house on the hill. He opened his hand and held it flat against the sky. "I own land," he said, "from here to the Barranca river and a mile north and south."

Indian Charlie searched the area for a stick. He

found one about three feet long. Near the road, he began to dowse but found no sign. A few minutes later, about fifty yards from Martin's house, the stick nearly bolted from Indian Charlie's hand.

"That it?"

Indian Charlie looked to them, "Come, Mr. Walters, and experience the water magic."

Martin held the rod and the Indian placed a hand on top of his. The rod jolted, and Martin yelled dropping the rod as if he were shocked. "Christ! It's like a thunderbolt," he said dancing out of control. "Make it go away."

"Hee. Hee."

"Come," said Indian Charlie. He wrapped his arms around Martin and pulled them both to the ground. "Roll," he said, "that is how you thank the water spirit." Clinging to each other, they rolled over and over in the dirt until the electricity went away.

Dusting himself off, Indian Charlie said, "I estimate the water to be fairly far down, possibly four fifty. It should run in at fifteen to twenty gallons a minute." As he spoke he broke the stick into four pieces and threw one piece toward each of the four winds. "It is a pleasure to do business with you. I will collect the remaining two hundred fifty when the driller proves that the water will not evade us."

"That's easier than I thought," said Martin. "Nice trick, Indian."

32. "that's why I shot him."

After it was over, most everyone agreed that it hadn't been meant to last for long. A couple who couldn't make it through a slow dance without running to the parking lot tearing at one another never did last for long.

Digger was a hot blooded drifter, and Purty tried to ride him out. He had been spending some of his time with an Indian woman in Gallup, some of his time with Estelle Anderson, and some of his time with the quick tricks in the Arsenal. He didn't spend much time with Purty, and she was plain fed up.

A half an hour before she shot him, she was walking past Chuck Swanson's Hardware. "Evening, Purty," Chuck had said. "If you are looking for Digger, he is out at the Arsenal."

"Whoosh," said Purty. "That Digger. Much obliged, Chuck."

She felt a fever sweep over her, she was thirsty, her head began to spin. She had felt the same way when they told her Lou was dead, the hot dizziness, the voices, the whirring in her brain.

"I should have done something a long time ago," she said. In her hotel room, she fumbled in the bureau and got the gun. When she slammed closed the drawer, the picture of Lou Willis fell to its face, she knew the glass had broken even without looking.

She arrived at the Arsenal out of breath, her eyes were on fire. Digger sat at the bar with a woman, they looked liquored up. She had one shoe off and was running her foot up and down his leg, he was fondling a medallion she had hung low on her neck. He tugged the medallion and she came in for a kiss.

When Purty showed up behind Digger waving the gun, the woman lurched backwards hard enough to break the medallion's chain. Her face was frozen in a scream.

"Lou Willis," said Purty evenly. "You are a dead man."

As Digger turned, the bullet struck him in the throat. He slumped onto the woman and spouted blood on her skirt long after Purty had gone.

She climbed the hotel stairs for the second time that night. She wrapped herself in a robe, and Sheriff Finch found her waiting for him.

III.

Chapter seven.

33. At the Mud Rocket.

"Have you noticed that the places around here sound dry," asked Pfizer. "Aguila, Alacran, Hueco, Calavera, Desert Wells, Culebra, Cojo, Pelado hill."

Quinn and Pfizer sat in canvas chairs in the dome room of the Mud Rocket. "I haven't any idea what those words mean," said Quinn.

The chemist, with a sparkle in his eye, answered with: "Here we go. Eagle, scorpion, hollow, skull, snake, lame man, bald. Hee. Hee."

"How do you do that?"

"Once you train your memory on the periodic tables in early youth, nothing is difficult after that."

"Bald Hill. I like Pelado hill," said Quinn looking outside down off the hill. "It doesn't sound so empty. Ha."

The sections in the lower portions of the dome were removable, and on warm days with the panels out, the room became much like a large umbrella. A breeze passed through the cool shade.

The Mud Rocket had no stairs, Quinn had built a ladder from cedar poles and stuck it through a hole in the ceiling. When anyone wanted privacy in the dome room, he could pull the ladder up behind him. Quinn had left the ladder down for Pfizer's visit.

Pfizer narrowed his eyes and looked at the younger man, narrowed his eyes as though he were looking into the wind. "It's pretty quiet out here compared with the city. Isn't it."

"Yes. I like the quiet."

"You must miss it sometimes." Pfizer prepared for Quinn's answer.

"A little."

"That's what I thought. You city people always do."

"I still don't know how long we can stay."

"Why's that."

"Money," said Quinn. "Have to go to work soon."

"You like it around here well enough to stay."

"Yes," said Quinn.

"Well, I'd be glad to keep an eye out for you."

"Appreciate it."

Cornelia climbed the ladder to the dome room. Seeing there were people there, she buttoned her blouse one button more and tugged at her shorts. Her body was tanned ready for summer.

"Why don't you dig graves?" said Cornelia. "The old grave digger was shot by his mistress."

Cornelia glanced at Pfizer. He was looking at her. He could not stop himself, her freshness bewildered him and made him stare.

"If I liked a man," she said, "I would be angry if he cheated on me. But I would never shoot him."

"Dig graves?" said Quinn. "Pfizer, what does that pay?"

"I believe Monatti was getting two dollars an hour for upkeep and twenty-five a grave. It isn't much, but your time is your own."

"Would you consider taking on that type of work?"

"I might."

"I will help you, Quinn. I have never dug a grave before."

Pfizer watched the girl. She smiled at him, the naturalness of her smile invited him to admire her without feeling embarrassed.

"Have you seen the bridge that Cornelia and Sergia have built, Pfizer. You should go down and see it."

"I would like that," said Pfizer getting up to go.

"Come on up again," said Quinn.

"I may take you up on that."

"Let me go down with you," said Cornelia. Barefoot, she scrambled down the ladder like a cat.

Pfizer caught up with her outside. "How did you build your bridge, Cornelia."

Cornelia answered, "You take several poles and fix them together with well spiked cross pieces and flatten the top to make for sure footing. Now, since an insecure railing is far worse than no railing at all, we built a sturdy one by peeling the bark off a pole and fitting it snug in the crotch of a tree on either side of the stream. You should come and walk across it some time."

"I would like that."

34. Dry hole melodrama.

"How does your drilling go?" asked Indian Charlie.

"Down four hundred feet and dry."

"The water is evading."

"Do you miss often, Indian."

"No. The water has never evaded the drill before."

"I'm out my two-fifty plus the drilling."

"That is true, Mr. Walters."

Indian Charlie sat quiet cross-legged in front of the Road Runner Shop wrapped in a blanket, his pottery bowl for change next to him, his postcards in a fan which he held high.

Almost as if it were a forewarning, the wind gusted down the narrow main street of Rio Barranca bringing with it fine sand, newspapers, and tumbleweed. One of the dry bushes glanced off Indian Charlie and tangled in Martin's feet.

"I know your kind, Indian," said Martin kicking away the clinging weed. "I seen what your kind do. I get a bad taste in my mouth from just talking to you."

Indian Charlie his smile wide and friendly held his cards up to a passerby who was struggling against the wind.

"Hey, Mr. Water Witch, I'm talking to you."

Indian Charlie continued to hold the fluttering postcards which were almost obscured by the dust.

"Hey! When Martin Walters talks, Indian, you listen." Martin clamped to the Indian's shoulder and began to try and lift him from the sidewalk.

With his free hand, Indian Charlie reached for Martin's wrist. "You must not treat me with violence," said the Indian calmly.

When Martin continued to try and lift Indian Charlie off the ground, the Indian repeated his warning and took his grip on Martin's wrist.

Martin went rigid. When Indian Charlie released him, he slumped against the building.

"Oh. Jesus," said Martin.

"You must not treat me with violence," Indian Charlie repeated the third time. "The water is evading."

"That bastard Indian has an electric wire attached to him," Martin mumbled as he staggered down the street toward Lupine's. "I've been shocked twice now by the son of a bitch."

35. Help wanted.

Robert Quinn came down off Pelado hill into Rio
Barranca and went directly to Lupine's. He had been
in the place a couple of times, but he had never
spoken to Lupine herself. The place was empty
except for Johnny Ouranous who was wiping
counters in the back. He mumbled to himself as he
wiped.

"You dug before, Mr. Quinn."

"No, Ma'am."

"Can you use a shovel?"

"Yes, Ma'am."

"You have to talk with Art Blackstone. If he
thinks it's all right, then you can consider yourself
hired. Good luck to you."

"Thank you, Ma'am."

"Lupine."

"Right. Thanks, Lupine."

As Quinn walked away, Lupine said to
Johnny O., "Mighty funny, a fellow like him

looking to dig graves. Not a bad looker, hey, Johnny."

Johnny Ouranous did not hear her, "Set Taylor Basin to the north. Climb Dead Indian Draw up to Greasy Creek. Five hundred yards northwest."

"Come to think of it, they are putting down old Wilber Luce on Tuesday. I might just wander up there myself. He taught me history once."

"Come on in, Young Fella," Art Blackstone was spreading clothes over a man when Quinn entered his office. The trousers were half trousers with strings that he tied behind the man's legs. The shirt was nothing more than a collar and bib just large enough to cover what the coat wouldn't. The tie was a clip-on.

"If he doesn't turn over," said Blackstone. "He won't know the difference. Ha."

"I heard you might be coming by, you're Robert Quinn. Am I right?"

"Right."

"Ever dug before?"

"No."

"Well, it's something you can learn. Come on in here and let's sit."

Blackstone led Quinn into the front section of his office. The chairs were comfortable, leather upholstery, the flowers used for both church and funeral were stuck in vases and bowls all about the room. A refrigerator in the far corner held carnations and roses.

"Now," said Blackstone. "The hardest thing about digging is getting it the right size all the way down. Some people think that making it down the six feet is the worse part. Well, you should have seen my first hole. It shot off on the bias and was so narrow they pretty nearly had to set the box in edgeways. As it was, they had to slide it along the side. Take it from me, make your edges straight, and go straight down. We like a tight fit in these parts, and remember when you dig, you aren't digging a hole, you're cutting one just like a knife in thick dough. Tie a stone to a piece of string the first couple of times, that will send you straight down."

"I own a plumb bob."

"A stone on a piece of string will do the trick. But, so much the better, use that the first couple of times." He examined him carefully. "Do you have a place to live. There's a shack up at the yard you can use if you want. Heard something about you living in an adobe hut north of town. Move in at the yard if you want to."

"It isn't exactly a hut. It's a house. We haven't any water or electricity yet, but we can live up there all right."

"Well, you take a walk up to the yard. The key is on the nail there." Blackstone got up from the chair and went back to the dressing and embalming room.

"You came just in time," he said. "Old Wilber Luce here is due to go down on Tuesday. Thought I would have to dig the hole myself." He turned and resumed work. "We pay two dollars an hour and twenty-five a grave to start. You dig it out and fill it in after the ceremony. Luce's plot is marked up in the northeast corner, you'll find it."

He was clearly fascinated with Blackstone's work.

"You had better get on up there. The first couple take quite a little while longer than you would expect." Blackstone turned and shook his hand. "If you feel like dropping in here sometime, feel free. We can always put you to work doing something."

Quinn said, "See you up at the yard on Tuesday."

"Say, Quinn. There's a shower in the shack. You might want to use it when you finish the hole."

36. Is it not sad to relate.

"Licket," said Lena Romero, her throat parched, "are you here?"

She got no answer and fell back into the bed's warmth, the canopy remained closed. The only comfortable position for her was flat on the back. "Mother of Christ," her voice rasped, "let me survive my scourge."

Rio Barranca, cobblestone streets clattering with wagons, cedar posts for fences, dust swirls. Lena saw a man, a stranger to her, stagger, red eyed, and fall into the gutter a roll of foam at his mouth.

Is it not sad to relate,
A Perfect Stranger to Rio Barranca
Died on this date.

Rigid, she saw from a porch stoop, Lou Willis, dead, his groin stained a brilliant red. Spasms shot through her back, the sores burned like acid, her buttocks felt as though a hot knife were searing through them where she sat on the edge of the porch stoop.

123

Is it not sad to relate,
Lou Willis, Stone Cutter,
Died on this date.

Vultures, kites, ravens and other strange fowl
passed over Rio Barranca in great numbers, their
croaking could be heard for miles. When they turned
suddenly to fly low over the town, their turning
shut out the sky. In the darkness, the people of Rio
Barranca began to cry for help.

Plow the town.

A widow seven years to plow the town.

"My Lady," said Licket, "I am sorry to be late." He
was wet from his swimming at the Rio Barranca
reservoir. "They are calling for you, My Lady. You
must help them."

Black veils, skirts, a wind hammering at the
unlatched doors. Lena Romero with six virgins, two
Indians, a rusty plow and a long stick of dead wood
walked to the outskirts of Rio Barranca, black storm
clouds concealed them. An Indian, the one who
would remain behind to stand guard, scribed a ring
with the stick. The women entered the ring and all
dropped their garments.

Naked before the wind. How young and ripe the
virgins, how joyously shy and like milk were they in
the dark light. The strength of their legs, the flair
of their hips, their breasts and proud faces. Purty
Romero was among them, strong and tall. To think,
Lena had a daughter clean to help her plow the

124

town. Lena watched her being harnessed to the
plow. The brown hands of the Indian touched her,
lingered at her waist.

Pressing the dead stick to the ground, Lena began
to scribe a circle around Rio Barranca. The six girls
followed, plowing to the mark.

Lena whispers back to Purty. Lower your eyes.
Purty is watching the town's people in their
windows, she can feel them looking at her. Proud,
she stands before them challenging with her flashing
eyes, her erect, firm body, their stares from the
darkened windows. Wind whips across their path
slashing Purty's hair. She faces the wind and throws
her head back, her hair lashing long and black at her
shoulders. Lena moves on slowly scribing the line
around Rio Barranca. The maidens except for one
strain against the plow. Lower your eyes. Pull your
load. Storm clouds leave the town in darkness.
Lower your eyes, Lena hissed in anger. The stick
snaps.

The broken stick fell to the dust, Lena covered her
face. Instantly, a pale blue fire danced on Purty's
lips. She hesitated, strained against the harness, and
fell to her knees. The Indian left the plow and came
forward to unhitch her. He rolled Purty to her back,
the blue fire played over lips and breasts, the Indian
cried out and backed away. Purty's legs fell open in
the dust. The blue fire danced around her thighs and
disappeared. A smile, then, appeared on Purty's lips,

and she stood. Sinuating, supple as a reed, she
moved her hands over her body displaying herself.
The people in the darkened windows gasped.
Gesturing for them all to come suckle. Laughing,
exhilarated, her eyes ablaze, she stepped from the
plow and disappeared into the shadow of a doorway.

> Is it not sad to relate,
> Lena Romero lost her daughter,
> Purty, on this date.

A throng of voices, calling like bells, sought
another maiden. Virgin. Virgin. The voices cried out
in the darkness. Have strength Lena Romero. Virgin.
Virgin.

"My Lady, you must go on," said Licket. He sat
alert at the end of her bed.

Once again they gathered outside of town at the
ring. All but one were naked, and she quickly
dropped her garments in the dust. Tears streaming
down her face, Lena trailed the dead stick around
Rio Barranca. Six virgins, harnessed to a plow, an
Indian with the reins, followed her. Where Lena's
tears fell, a gentle current rose from the earth and
turned about the maidens. A steam, they said, that
soothed their chafed shoulders and their weary legs.

"Oh, Licket," she moaned, her throat dry, before
passing once again into a deeper sleep.

"Rest now, My Lady. Rest." said Licket until he
saw her hands relax.

Chapter eight.

37. The musk hog metamorphosis.

i

"Sorry, Martin. It's no good," said Estelle as he got
out of his pickup truck and walked toward the pit
at the snake museum. There he saw them lying limp
and motionless, and he blanched at the sight. Estelle
allowed him to bury his head in the nape of her
neck and she led him inside the trailer house.

"They were my last living memory of her,
Estelle," Martin's voice had completely broken.

"I know," said Estelle. She knew how to care for
Martin. At least she thought she knew how to help
him forget, and she discovered that she was eager to
do it.

"Even the rattlers were quiet," said Estelle.
"When I used the poke, Ouroboros struck alone to
protect the others. I did everything I could. They
decided to give up the fight, Martin. When they decide
to do that, nobody can get them to turn back."

Martin's eyes were moist. He slumped on the sofa in a daze. She went to him and sat close. She held his head against her bosom. She was powdered and freshly perfumed. "I tried everything."

Martin's tears were dampening Estelle's front, her tattoo had begun to show through her white uniform. "You really did love those snakes, didn't you." Her compassion was pungent.

"Don't bury them," he could hardly speak. His throat was tight, he might have been gagging. "Get them skinned and mounted for me. I want to put them in the museum."

She touched one of his tearstains on her dress. The red and dark blue of the tattoo showed through the dress. She pressed him against her and lifted his hand to her breast. She began to unbutton her uniform.

"It's been too long. Hasn't it, Martin." She turned on the radio. "Remember the Savoy? Jenny was away somewhere then too."

"Just get them skinned. I'll tack them to the boards myself." Martin's eyes were red, and he could not see.

"Oh. Martin. It goes like this. Didn't it, Honey. Remember."

ii

The following morning Martin woke up in his bed at his home and found that he had been almost entirely metamorphosed.

130

His head and body, three feet, tail one foot, twenty inches at the shoulder, he weighed from forty-five to fifty pounds. He had a coat of a stiffish black-brown hair, with a white band on his shoulders, and he had an erectile crest from crown to rump.

He tends to like to live in small herds, ten to twelve at most. When a herd is brought to bay they stand in close formation, champing tusks and making determined charges. It is reputed that if one of the herd is attacked the rest come to its aid. However, if he finds himself utterly alone, he takes to holes in the ground if they are available.

He will eat almost anything animal or vegetable, but seems to prefer mainly roots, fruits, and grains.

iii

Martin was a busy man those last few days, he methodically:

1. Sold the buffalo to a curio complex on Route Sixty-four near Santa Fe and leased the land to a curious stranger who called himself Feather River Joe. The house trailer went along with the deal.

2. Paid Chico Mendez's kid brother for skinning the rattlers which he mounted on slabs of varnished plywood.

3. Painted an X in white through the huge bill-boards which read *Rattlers' Nest, Cactus Cool Ade, Curios, Snakes Live!* and had been set up along the

roads out of Las Vegas, Dallas, Denver, and
Cleveland to guide travelers to Rio Barranca.

4.   Unlocked the door to his bomb shelter which
he had not been in since the mid-fifties and found
that the room was dank. A green moss had grown
over the ceiling bulb which exploded into its
protective wire mesh when Martin turned on the
light switch.

"Son of a bitch," said Martin. His voice was
hollow in the cement shell. He replaced the bulb
and checked the emergency rations, first aid
equipment, shotgun. The room was not luxurious,
but it was comfortable. A folding cot, chair,
standing lamp, moldy carpet, refrigerator, radio,
television, a rack of paperback books, mysteries and
westerns.

He turned on the heater to dry the place out and
aired the carpet. He hauled everything, all the
mementos of Izella the Snake Lady from the relic
corner of the snake museum and his office to the
shelter, the display cases, posters, mounts, skins,
everything. They took more room than he had
estimated, and he had to remove the television,
radio, and the rack of paperbacks before the
museum would fit.

5.   Sat alone in a straight-back chair holding a
bottle of whiskey and gazing into the flames. When
the main building of the snake museum was gutted,
he threw the half empty bottle into the fire and
went away.

A radio blared over the empty landscape. Estelle Anderson was in her trailer. A horse with a split ear, its head buried in a feed bag, was hitched outside.

6.   Scattered some tumbleweeds on the steps leading down to the bomb shelter's steel door to cover his tracks.

7.   Threw the bolt and secured it with a padlock.

8.   Removed the key from his key ring and carefully mutilated the teeth with a hammer.

38. Desperate dreams.

The rushing sound of the Barranca river filled the evening in Pfizer's room. He sat alone smoking a long stem pipe, listening to the rush of the river.

He gradually became aware of a place in his mind, a circle of light, an arena in early morning, a moss place in a grove. Cornelia walked through the circle and turned, she was nude. She came to Pfizer, she came to see him, to talk with him, to make love. She was very gentle and soft with him, she could sit quietly for a long time. She could be completely quiet and create a silence that made him feel as though he were alone in a forest but with her. She was so gentle, he believed she was moss, and soft grass, and warm wind, and the first person he had ever made love with. She made him breathe quickly, she made his eyes see differently, she made him soft and aroused at once. They sat quietly and talked even when they were silent. When he touched her

cheek her entire body responded. She kissed him
and felt him. Pfizer's ejaculation took him by
surprise. She receded to wait until he had rested.
Her body was very beautiful, and he liked the way
it amazed him. She became transported, and he felt
he kissed her mind. He could see the colors and
patterns his lips made. He liked being loved as a
scientist, touched by someone who seemed to like
small things, and tight patterns the way he did.

39. Feather River Joe.

A horseman came riding down County Route Nine.
Three hills away he appeared to be floating, trotting
on a dust cloud. Less starched than the drugstore
fellows, he was a jovial, mannered, lanky, cowboy
with string hair loose under his hat, six-shooters,
chaps, leather vest, and a right eye that was locked
in position.

He originated in the city like most cowboys and
had come west with no more than his guns and
horse. He didn't like to act mean, but would stop a
man, freeze him in his tracks, if he was forced into
it. He rolled his own cigarettes from a greasy cloth
bag, and his shiny revolvers glistened in the sun
light.

Lupine flatly wouldn't let him in her place, she
didn't want a bullet hole in her floor. He rode right
through Rio Barranca and out to Pelado hill. The
first thing he said was, "The people are in their
chairs. I am Feather River Joe. My shit stinks. This

136

horse is called Wind. He got his ear split in a gun fight in Omaha."

Quinn said, "Glad to meet you. We were just having a bit of supper. Come in. If it suits you, stay and eat."

"Mighty good rice," he said to Katie his mouth full.

"Mighty kind of you," said Katie.

"I got three small incisors, one large canine, one cheek-tooth on each side in both my lower and upper jaw. I am used to small rabbits, a carrion or two, some vegetables and fruit, occasionally I will have the suckling young of some domestic stock. Rice is a nice change."

"We will have some fruit later on," said Katie.

When he was full, Feather River leaned back in his chair. "Well, I got me some land leased," he said puffing out, "with a cement block building on it gutted by fire and a trailer. How would you turn a fast buck with it, if you were me?" Feather River Joe looked at Sergia. She returned a warm smile. "What do you think, Button Nose."

"Why don't you open a roadside stand," said Katie.

"What kind would you suggest, Ma'am."

"A sea shell stand," said Sergia quickly.

He tilted his hat back and rubbed his jaw, speculating.

They all nodded, speculating with him.

"There isn't one around," said Quinn.

"Well, I guess I might as well get to it. Yup.

Thanks for the rice, Ma'am."

Feather River Joe got up from the table. "If you don't act a little impulsive at times, many a worthwhile plan drifts away like dinner table chatter." He pulled down his hat. "Good evening, Ladies. You all will be seeing me soon."

He went to his horse. "Get your dog-darn head out of that feed bag," he said, "we got to get to a telephone."

He sprung to his horse and galloped off down the hill, "Live shrimp. Giant Clam Shells. Barnacles. Poison Eels. Sea Horses," he yelled disappearing into the darkness.

"Who was that man," asked Sergia.

"Feather River Joe," Quinn answered.

40.   Bicycle Lena free from stain.

Without heed of what is decent or indecent the
people live guided only by their instincts, and do by
day or night alone or in company, whatever their
inclination may prompt them. And it is not only
the laity who behave thus, but the nuns in the
convents also, neglecting their rules, abandon
themselves to carnal lust, and deem that by
voluptuousness and excess they will prolong their
lives. (Giovanni Boccaccio, 1353)

The canopy on the bed remained closed. Lena's eyes
were open, small and red like rat's eyes. She looked
into the half light and saw them walking towards
her. She saw their long hair, their long beards, their
black hats, and she smiled.

Tell us. Plead for mercy and deny your attach-
ment to the Devil.

Tell us. Break all ties and declare your everlasting
love for the Divine.

Tell us.

I have received succor from those in the dark place. I have on my breast a scarred cross. I will tell you. The evil one comes to me for nourishment. I open my body to him, I make the sign of homage.

Tell us. Free yourself from stain.

I will tell you, said Lena. Please take away the pain.

The men leaned toward her, their long black beards, their tall hats, formed a black wall surrounding her. Their eyes pierced her heart.

I will tell you. He came to me first in a dream. I was young and lying in a sunny open field. He whispered for me to go to the herder's cottage and to live there three days washing in the stream cleaning and combing myself for him. He said that he would return to me on the third night.

Oh, it hurts me. Take away the pain. He did not come to me a second time. I had obeyed him and I had not eaten and movement was difficult for me. I was dizzy and breathing very quickly. He was dressed entirely in black, he was handsome. He undressed before the bed and told me to kiss him and to make the sign of homage. He then had intercourse with me. He lay with me for one entire night. In the morning he was gone.

Oh, the pain lightens. For two weeks, I waited for a sign. I could not sleep, I could not eat, for love I could not stop myself from returning to the cottage, aching for him to come again.

As before, he returned to me on the third night.

140

He promised to be my loving husband until death and to avenge me of my enemies.

I promised to be his loving faithful wife. Again, he was gone when I awoke. I had my child by him, and she does not love me.

> By Mary's honour free from stain,
> Arise and do not sin again.

Gloved hands lifted her and carried her to the square. She refused the manacles. Red-hot rods, six, glowed in the fire. Six times she was torn. Six times she pressed her cheek to the steel's heat. Six times the bearded men nodded as she leaned to the glowing irons.

> Bicycle Lena free from stain,
> Arise and do not sin again.

No one was familiar to her then. She had been lifted away, and now she could finally rest, her fever broken.

41. Cactus Cool Ade.

Signs began to pop up along the road leading to Rio Barranca, whitewash on plywood, teaser signs, which read: *Sea Horses, Live Shrimp, Man Eating Clam, Sharks' Teeth.*

Inside the shell house, the steel beams were slightly warped from the earlier fire, but the roof of corrugated steel was new and strong. A few small aquariums held fish, turtles, a squid. And shells, millions of shells in wooden crates covered the concrete floor and rough wood tables. "Stingaree. Stingaree. Shave yourself with a razor back clam. Eat soup with a scallop shell." Feather River Joe in buccaneer outfit, boots, tri-cornered hat, brandishing a swordfish jaw carried on a patter all day whether there were customers in the shell house or not. "Coral bells. Wind chimes. Cork. Stingaree. Stingaree. Run your best friend through with this genuine, authentic jaw bone of a swordfish caught in the Pacific ocean."

142

Crates lined the entrance, crates filled with authentic silver and turquoise Indian jewelry, Indian pottery, headdresses, bows and arrows, drums. "Stingaree, Buckaroo. Ride a genuine cowboy pony for twenty-five cents." Mexican tinware, beaded belts, moccasins, Indian costumes, wineskins. The cement block building was filled. Wind, his head in a feed bag was tethered to a tractor wheel in back.

"I don't know what I would have done if you and your old stud horse hadn't come along, Feather River. Why, when I saw the flames and crazy Martin sitting out there with his whiskey bottle, I thought I might as well go jump in and let the fire consume me."

"Think nothing of it, Estelle."

"I will not think nothing of it. I am grateful to you, Feather River. And, I plan to show you how grateful I am."

"My pleasure, Estelle. Think nothing of it."

"I will do no such thing," said Estelle.

Feather River said, "You give a man a fine dinner, Estelle. Every time I go up to that Mud Rocket, it seems we have rice. Those people must have rice twenty times a week. Hell, I don't mind it. But rice with garlic, rice with celery, rice with beans. It drives a man bull shit. They must live cheap, but it ain't nothing like this, Estelle. You sure give a man a fine dinner."

"But before I show you how grateful I am Feather River, I want to ask you one little favor.

143

I know how nice you are to let me run the cash register. I have one more little request." She turned on the radio and went over toward him moving slowly to the music. "We can do the dishes later."

Feather River said, "Dog darn, Estelle. You are direct. Did you ever try getting a piece of ass off one of them women up there. Hell, you know. All I want is a simple old fuck."

"Why, from the moment you came along, astride that pony, I could tell that, Feather River. I could tell you weren't no cowpoke who couldn't get it up. I could tell you were a wrangler. You are a real wrangler in my book, Feather River."

"Those crazy dames don't see it. They got to look deep in your eyes. Check how sensitive you are. Buzz around in your head. Hell, by the time they finished their God damn mind show, I am plumb tuckered. Grounds a man's battery, it does. Oh, you sure are direct, Estelle."

"Feather River, Honey. Look here. Hands away, Mister." She pushed herself against the steel pole in the trailer's living room. "Let me ask you one little favor." Estelle rubbed against the pole and began moving her hands over her body. "Could we have. I mean, would you let me add one little old thing to the shell house."

Feather River said, "Hot damn, Estelle. Every time you do that I like it better. You are so direct, like a shot of whiskey."

"I would like it if we had a juice bar. Then, I could sell Cactus Cool Ade. It's my own recipe. You serve it in the cutest glasses that look like a Saguaro cactus. They love it, they really do. It's a thirst quencher."

"Sure, Estelle, sure." His body began to move in sympathy with hers.

"Thank you, Feather River."

She turned the radio higher and flung herself at the pole rubbing and caressing herself with it. "Hands away, Mister. Don't touch until the lady asks." She danced strong. "And, when she does ask, Mister, you better hang on, for you are going to get the ride of your life."

"Oh, Estelle," said Feather River. "You sure are direct."

Chapter nine.

42. Licket's last stick.

Through the bed's canopy, Bicycle Lena saw a light
that looked very much like a burning bulb that
someone was swinging in the room. She lifted the
canopy for the first time in days and saw before her
Dr. Dee's brilliant light ring.

"It looks like that's it. Let me say before the last
stick that it has been mighty pleasant here in Rio
Barranca. I wouldn't have missed it for the world.
I don't usually feel that way about a place, and you
can bet I've been around some."

Licket walked toward a cedar stick resting by the
bank of the reservoir. "Well, I'm off. Let me just
give that stick there a toss." He held one end lightly
in his jaws and flipped the piece of cedar a fair
distance out in the reservoir.

The light ring began to grow dimmer and it hovered
over Lena's bed.

"Oh, Dr. Dee," said Lena. "Don't let's play games. Come here to me." Lena had not spoken so many words aloud for so long that the sound of her voice surprised her.

Licket, taking a few steps back up the bank, ran full speed to the edge of the reservoir. He stopped abruptly and leapt, weightless, in a graceful arch toward the floating stick.

"Well, I'll see you," he said through clenched teeth.

And, Licket began to swim in a close circle, increasing his speed, swimming faster and faster, setting up the current. Then, this took a surprisingly short time, he stopped swimming altogether and vanished in the whirlpool.

A few minutes later, the stick bobbed to the surface, and the reservoir returned to normal. A slight breeze swept through the cedar trees, and the waves carried Licket's stick back to shore.

So long, Licket! Thanks.

43. The Taylor Basin Lode spasm.

Johnny Ouranous came out of Lupine's into the dry
morning air for a sit and a smoke in the sun. He
wore his hat tilted back and sat motionless, the
smoke curling around his fingers.

"Howdy, Johnny," said Pfizer passing by.

Pfizer had gone two or three paces before
realizing that Johnny Ouranous had not only
returned the salutation but was actually calling to
him.

"I say, Mr. Lawrence."

No one had had a conversation with Johnny
Ouranous for years.

"You know Indian Charlie, don't you?"

Pfizer nodded.

"I have been thinking. If he can locate water, he
can locate veins, mineral veins." Johnny's cobalt
eyes flashed. "I never told anybody up to now, Mr.
Lawrence. Remember them rich samples I brought
in to you five or six years back?"

Pfizer remembered.

"They came from the Taylor Basin Lode. I am sure of it. If Indian Charlie can locate veins, I might just see if he would go partners." Johnny looked away from Pfizer off north to the mountains. "I left the jeep that day and walked. Set Taylor Basin to the north. Climb Dead Indian Draw up to Greasy Creek. Five hundred yards northwest. And, that's where I always lose it. Must have gone back there more than twenty times. I always lose it in the same place. Just that far from the biggest lode in this country."

"It was a dry hole out at Martin's place, Johnny."

"A dry hole?" The recklessness, the gambler's flashing in his eyes, vanished. He turned dark again, he was swept back, closing doors as he went. Johnny O. sat down on the bench and nodded to Pfizer. "Much obliged."

Sitting motionless, legs crossed underneath his apron, he let the smoke curl around his fingers. The cigarette burned to where he could feel its heat, and without looking he tossed it to just about the same place he usually tossed his burned-down butts.

44. *Datura* (three).

At noon, Ingrid Bloomstrom closed the Road
Runner Shop for two hours and bathed in the sun.
She went to Ernie Hinkle's with a blush of red on
her chest and legs. She smelled of a healthy mixture
of perfume and tanning lotion.

Ernie had a cement-block building north of Rio
Barranca on the Red Mesa road. The steel beams
were exposed as well as the pipes and the gas
blower. The floor was concrete and had a drain.
Workbenches of unfinished lumber and plywood
lined one wall. The far end, a drawer safe in the
corner held the jewelry, silver, and stones, a few
folding aluminum chairs, a cot, and Ernie's desk.
The building wasn't large, the high ceiling made it
seem large.

He showed her his anvil, his furnace, his cold
chisels, his files, his casting stones, his plaster. He
showed her how he could make fifty bracelets and
twenty rings and as many concho belts without

retooling or even sharpening the dies. He did a little hand stamping for her, he turned on the polishing and cutting machines for her. He let her work the grinder and press a disk. He had her witness how he kept his machines in good, clean condition. He had her witness his knowledge of profit margin.

"I had to take some of the things to Gallup for a show," he said turning his back to shelter her from the safe combination.

"Oh," she said as he pulled open the safe drawers. "That's what I like."

"I want you to have this," said Ernie holding a small silver ankle bracelet with a bell on it.

She rang the bell close to her ear and delighted in the soft tinkle. Ernie looked away as she bent down to put the bracelet on her bare ankle.

And, he was completely taken by surprise, and couldn't help but wonder, if only for a fleeting moment, if she had not taken some *datura* before he had picked her up that evening, as she was gently taking his face in her hands and kissing him warm and full on his mouth saying, "Oh, Ernie."

45. Muslin clouds.

The dry wind swept like fire over the graveyard
bending the tall grass sucking what little moisture
remained from the hard red soil. The sky was a
wash of deep blue. Katie in a long muslin dress
walked toward the hole Quinn was working on in
the far corner of the cemetery. She carried a
radiance with her, an exhilaration. Her long hair
braided in a single plait down her back, her blue
eyes as blue as the sky.

"Hey, I brought you something," she said peering
down at him, shirtless, perspiring.

He looked up at her. The red bandana tied
around his head was soaked, he had to wipe the
sweat out of his eyes to see. She stood with the sun
at her back.

"You look like a cloud today, Kate." His voice
echoed in the hole. "Toss that ladder in here for
me, will you."

She found a short ladder not far from the hole

and lowered it. He climbed out of the grave and kneeling reached down to pull the ladder out after him. "Ought to get a rope with a hook on it," he said tossing the ladder onto the dirt pile.

They looked at each other and smiled, they looked into one another's eyes and for both of them the world fell away. They each had the sensation that if they were to stop looking at each other for a moment and were to look around them they would instantly find themselves standing high, alone, and frightened on an obelisk, the world far below. They looked at one another without fear.

"Hello, Kate."

"Hello, Robert."

They kissed to break the spell. Their kisses always broke spells just as their loving always finished conversations rather than began them.

She ran to sit on a white marble monument. "Come here," she said.

"There it is," said Quinn walking toward her. "My first one. Hope the box fits."

He saw her white muslin dress. "What did you bring me?"

She spread her hands on her belly. He saw flashes of color there in the white. Like magic they appeared, patches of light and bright spires in the circle of her white belly.

He took a deep breath. "I don't think I can stand it," he said kissing her again.

"I thought you could tell by how bitchy I have been."

"I did sort of. Not really. How would I know?"

They sat close to each other. "And, I know just when it happened."

"So do I." She was deliriously radiant.

"I knew it. I should have stayed and fished that day."

"Well. Alameda isn't a bad name."

"Are you certain?" asked Quinn.

"I wanted to tell you before the growing starts, so you wouldn't be taken by surprise."

Quinn said, "I wasn't present when you began to develop breasts. In some places, when a girl begins, the boys run to her singing and rub her body with grease and ocher. They inscribe lines down her back and draw circles around her nipples."

He went to the pile of red dirt and brought a handful back. "That was their couvade," he said. He placed his hands softly on her belly. The red clay smeared on her muslin dress. He gently wrapped her in his arms and let out a wild cowboy yell in sheer delight.

The wind took his yell and whipped it all the way down to the valley of the Barranca river and beyond.

couvade - A practice among certain primitive people in which the husband of a woman in labor takes to his bed as if he were bearing the child.

157

46. Dreams come true.

The two girls bronze as Indians, naked as boys, came up behind him. Cornelia's blonde hair was in a braid. Sergia's hung long and loose over her freckled breasts. They both wore only an apron-like garment which tied at the side so that when they walked the cloth fell open up their thighs.

Pfizer watched the proud swaying of their bodies and thought they looked wonderful walking hand in hand. Their backs were smooth and young. He didn't speak to either of them when he caught up to and passed them on the road, and he didn't dare look back.

"I went to him once," said Cornelia.

"He hasn't called me," said Sergia. "I would like to be with him sometime."

"He made me feel very nice."

"I think he is a good person. If you let him, he

will look into your mind a little. It is exciting and he is very gentle."

"I would like to let him be with me. It is always very good that way."

"I am happy for you, Cornelia."

"He will want you soon."

"Thank you, Cornelia."

A Trailways Bus sped by. Three white sailor hats smashed against the rear windows. The girls had turned and were waving.

Pfizer walked by the cultivated garden patches, the falling down barn that was built before Quinn's time on the land, an old car. He found they had set up a teepee, and he looked inside. A shaft of sunlight shattered on his forehead. He smiled at Cornelia and Sergia inside.

Pfizer crossed the field and began to walk back toward Rio Barranca. Further along, they came up behind him once again. They wore long skirts and soft blue blouses and seemed to melt into the sky. They drifted along the ridge following a deer trail which eventually led to the stream which fed the reservoir. Cornelia looked back and motioned for him to follow them. The trail was steep to the stream, and Pfizer's shoes slid on the grass and pine needles.

"Hello," said Sergia when Pfizer came up behind her. She was playing her fingers in the stream.

"Hello," said Pfizer.

Cornelia came to Pfizer. She kissed him. Sergia turned and faced him, she kissed him as well. They both removed their dresses while they stood before him. Cornelia began unbuttoning Pfizer's shirt. Sergia did his shoes. Their hands were gentle. Sergia's were still slightly cool from the water.

They led Pfizer to the pool where they bathed and swam. "This is our bridge," said Sergia. "We built it from two logs fastened together." She put her hand on the smooth peeled pole that was the railing. "Feel how sturdy it is," she said.

Pfizer walked across the bridge. "It is very sturdy," he said his hand on the railing.

Pfizer walked to the reservoir, and enjoying the freshness and quiet of the cool afternoon wind, he picked up a used chewed stick at the water's edge and tossed it far out on the calm water.

He found them both sitting in their long dresses on his swing. They had been watching him walk down the road. They were pretending to read a magazine.

He said nothing to them, he didn't even nod. He crossed the porch and quickly went inside.

The two girls waited a few moments. They left the swing, and after pressing nose and breasts against the window, their blouses tight, they followed him inside, letting the screen door slam shut behind them.

What a nice book.
Strikes me as more tender
and less-gimicky than
Braustijon. The magic
of Marquez.
T. Glover
2-8-73